"We Have [KU-533-644] of the Farmer's Daughter and the City Slicker.

Surely I deserve a chance to try it out." He circled around her, and she found herself backing toward the fallen hay.

"Aha, me beauty!" He twirled an imaginary mustache. "This time you won't get away, my sweet." His weight and a foot thrust behind her ankle brought them toppling over into the sweet-smelling hay.

"Oof! You great lout," she panted. "Mitch!" Her cry was smothered in a kiss. When he raised his head and smiled down at her triumphantly, a wave of emotion swept over her, making her shiver.

"Kathryn!" He was instantly contrite. "Did I hurt you?"

"Oh, Mitchell," she whispered. "Kiss me again." She didn't wait for him. Reaching up, she slid her fingers into his hair and pulled his head down to her waiting mouth, kissing him with abandon.

PAULA CORBETT

is a native of California but now lives in Boston, where she owns a successful antique business. Her wit and warm, quirky characters are sure to earn her a place among your favorite romance authors.

PAULA CORBETT
Maid In Boston

Silhouette Desire

Originally Published by Silhouette Books
division of
Harlequin Enterprises Ltd.

First published in Great Britain in 1985
by Mills & Boon Ltd, 15–16 Brook's Mews, London W1A 1DR

© Paula Corbett 1984

Silhouette, Silhouette Desire and Colophon are Trade Marks
of Harlequin Enterprises B.V.

ISBN 0 373 48623 5

0285

Made and printed in Great Britain by
Richard Clay (The Chaucer Press) Ltd,
Bungay, Suffolk

To Betsy

Maid In Boston

1

I told you, Miss Lambert. She don't want to go in!"

"Nonsense, Charlie. Our Betsey's only shy, aren't you, darling? After all, it's the first time, isn't it?"

Sparkling blue eyes looked coaxingly into huge, soft brown eyes surrounded by incredibly long lashes. Just when it seemed that the brown eyes were going to give in to the blue, a noise farther down the line of milking stations distracted Betsey. With a panicked "Moooo" of protest the cow backed cumbersomely away from the young woman who was sweet-talking her.

Kathryn Lambert, exasperated, leaned hard on the animal's side in an effort to halt its retreat. Almost pushed off her feet in the unequal contest, she threw her arm around Betsey's neck and dug in her heels.

"Come on, you great cow! Cooperate, won't you?" Panting with exertion, Kathryn felt another button give way on the worn checked blouse she'd put on that morning for work in the dairy barn.

"What's the matter with you, Charlie? Give her a swat on the rump!"

The swat was applied, but not by Charlie. Charlie was standing to one side, gaping at the darkly handsome, well-dressed man who had entered the barn and, unnoticed, joined the little group. Dusting his hands together lightly, the stranger smiled with satisfaction as Betsey walked meekly into the milking station.

Kathryn tore her eyes away from the unknown man and called to Charlie, "Don't just stand there. Get her hooked up before she changes her mind again."

Her assistant moved to do as she ordered, casting a quick glance at the stranger, who watched with interest as Charlie attached the mechanical fingers. The machine began to work on the cow's distended udder, and Betsey rolled her soft brown eyes at Kathryn.

Smiling in sympathy, Kathryn gave her an encouraging pat. "Never mind, love. You'll get used to it soon enough."

"That's a pity." There was amusement in the smooth, deep voice. "Mechanical fingers can hardly feel as good as human ones. I don't blame her for being so reluctant."

Kathryn put her hands on her hips as she swung around to face the stranger. Seeing the look of evident enjoyment that came over his face, she looked down and thought, Damn! The last button that popped had been a crucial one, and now her neckline gaped open, revealing the edge of her lacy bra and two rounded half moons of firm flesh.

"Yes," he continued, a glint appearing in the thickly lashed green eyes, "I would very much prefer the human touch."

Kathryn lowered her hands from her hips, hoping for a slight increase in strategic coverage. "You're referring to the cow, I hope." Her cool tone and direct blue gaze were a clear warning signal. Charlie, hovering nearby, snickered audibly, and Kathryn turned on him. "Why don't you get back to those new calves? Betsey will be fine now."

Though obviously sorry to leave just when things were getting interesting, Charlie shuffled off down the row of stalls. At the barn entrance he encountered a strongly built, ruddy-faced older man, who clapped him on the shoulder.

"Howdy, Charlie. How goes it?"

"Hey, boss. When did you get back?"

"Nate!" Kathryn's clear voice rose with pleasure. "We didn't expect you back 'til tomorrow."

She ran to meet her beaming uncle, who was already striding toward her. She flung her arms around his neck and kissed him soundly. "Nate, you look wonderful! I can't wait to hear what your Outward Bound trek was like." She ruffled his iron gray hair. "You probably taught more survival tricks than you learned."

"He certainly did." The stranger joined them, his eyes warm with admiration as he looked at the older man. "If it hadn't been for your uncle and a stout length of rope, I wouldn't be alive. I'd be lying at the foot of a mountain, permanently outward bound."

The two men exchanged a look of comradeship. Then Nate turned to Kathryn. "Honey, meet Mitchell Grant. He's from Boston, and we teamed up on the trek. Don't let his fancy duds fool you. Mitch is a great trailmate. I told him my niece was the prettiest female this side of the Green Mountains."

Despite Nate's proud smile, Kathryn winced inwardly. Both men surveyed her as though she were a small girl being shown off for company. Her uncle's eyebrows shot up when he noticed the missing buttons, but he made no comment. Mitchell took full advantage of the invitation to look her over again.

Slightly above medium height at five feet seven, Kathryn showed her Scottish descent in her pale, lightly freckled complexion and her candid blue eyes. The high, clearly defined cheekbones, pointed chin, and healthy skin free of makeup gave her face a piquant look and a freshness that belied her twenty-four years. The youthfulness was exaggerated by the long braids of auburn hair that hung down over her shoulders.

But there was nothing childish about her figure. The shapeliness of her bosom was not in question. The path Mitchell Grant's interested eyes now followed traced the womanly curves and long slender legs that were shown to advantage in her snug-fitting, faded jeans. Kathryn thought he just might ask her to turn around to complete the picture, and a bubble of half-offended amusement rose within her.

"Pleased to meet you, Mr. Grant." She gave way to temptation and said, her expression friendly and oh, so guileless, "I have no trouble at all picturing you hanging from the end of a rope."

His green eyes flew back to her face. After a second's pause, he said, "My pleasure, Miss Lambert."

"You don't have a Boston accent," she remarked.

"If I have an accent, it's a California one. I'm a transplant from the silicon valley of Santa Clara."

"The computer belt?"

"Yes, but Boston has its own computer industry."

Her uncle interjected to add, "Mitch has his own software firm. I told him you'd show him your computer operation here after lunch. First I want to give him a tour of an authentic Vermont dairy." He moved down the long rows of milking stations as he talked. "It's only recently that the people outnumber the cows in Vermont, Mitch. Three hundred thirty-nine thousand cows to half a million people, at last count."

They entered a huge room filled with stainless steel and glass and porcelain fixtures. Mitchell raised his voice to be heard over the hum of equipment. "What volume do you handle, Nate?"

"Kathryn's figures can tell you exactly, but it runs

about two thousand gallons a day. Three hundred head and rising. Mostly Holsteins, with some Jerseys."

As the men talked, Kathryn examined Mitchell more closely. Tall, strikingly handsome, he looked every inch the young businessman. Fitness conscious, too, she guessed. The fabric of his clothes stretched snugly over muscled shoulders and thighs, though he stood relaxed, his hands in his pockets.

Probably about thirty. Old enough to have acquired an aura of perfect assurance. Everything about him projected the kind of dynamic, aggressive qualities she automatically distrusted. The broad shoulders seemed to thrust forward. His square chin and strongly carved nose gave his face a look of determination and alertness. Even his hair contributed to the effect, cut and combed in an untamed kind of way, as though deliberately toning down a too-handsome face. She knew instinctively that he was a man who knew what he wanted and wouldn't miss any opportunity to get it.

He turned and caught her staring at him. Amused, he moved toward her as Nate gave instructions to a technician.

"From what I'm hearing, Miss Lambert, being a milkmaid these days isn't as easy as it used to be."

The condescension in his voice annoyed her. "I doubt if it ever was. Certainly not as easy as sitting in an office and giving other people orders all day."

"I don't actually do that. Any more than you spend your whole day getting reluctant cows into milking stalls."

Kathryn shrugged. "I work with the computer a lot, but it will seem small potatoes to an expert. We're really just novices."

"No harm in comparing notes," he said equably. "I'm always ready to learn what I can, even from novices." A provocative light gleamed in his green eyes.

She returned his look unblushingly. "I'm sure there's nothing a farm girl could teach you, Mr. Grant."

Nate rejoined them to lead their tour through another large barn and the veterinarian station, and on past a row of tall feed silos and other storage units. Mitchell looked with interest at a completely equipped garage where a tractor was being repaired. "It's a lot more complex than I expected," he remarked.

"Yes," Nate agreed. "Things have changed a lot since my father ran the dairy with one barn and thirty cows."

Mitchell's aristocratic nose twitched as he sniffed the fragrant air around them. "Some things don't change."

Nate laughed and clapped Mitchell on the shoulder. "Too true. But we never notice it, do we, Kathryn?"

Kathryn breathed in deeply. The ineradicable, earthy aroma was as familiar and pleasant to her as it was offensive to Mitchell, no doubt. She ignored his amused expression. "If you want lunch, I think we'd better go up to the house now. 'Manda's fixing lamb stew today, and a special dessert."

"We'll be along in a minute. I expect you want to change." The hint in Nate's voice was as close as he would come to commenting on the state of her shirt, which she had been holding closed with one discreetly placed hand. "I want to show Mitch a bit more of our setup, so he can see what our computer system is dealing with."

Kathryn felt strangely reluctant to leave them. Disquieted by Mitchell's effect on her, she opted for teasing him. "Nate usually brings back some trophy from his travels, Mr. Grant, but I must say this is the first time he's bagged a businessman."

"Kathryn!" Nate admonished, throwing a quick glance at Mitch, who grinned broadly. Satisfied that his irrepressible niece had not offended their guest, Nate called after her as she swung cheerfully away toward the farmhouse. "We've got a proposition to put to you, honey! So don't go making any plans for this afternoon, okay?"

"What," Kathryn muttered to herself as she hurried along, "is Uncle Nate up to now?"

After lunch Kathryn followed Amanda Lambert to the kitchen. Her aunt was a spare, peppery lady in her fifties, an excellent match for her energetic husband. The men had taken their second cups of coffee out onto the back verandah and 'Manda now regarded her niece with disapproval. "Just what do you think you're doing, Kathryn?"

"Helping you, of course," Kathryn replied innocently.

"I don't need any help. Get yourself out on the verandah. Nate told me he's got something he wants to talk to you about with his guest." She regarded her niece with critical eyes. "What did you want to put on that old pullover and skirt for? You want that Boston man to think our girls don't know how to dress properly when there's company?"

"I'm dressed like a farmer's daughter. That's just what he expects. It would only amuse him to see me dress like anything else."

"With those braids wrapped 'round your head and not a scrap of makeup on, he's going to think you herd the cows," 'Manda snorted. "You don't dress like that when Tom Wells comes to take you out."

"For heaven's sake, he's only here for lunch."

"Take your coffee out there and be friendly. Don't get up to any of your tricks. No stranger is going to tolerate that queer sense of humor of yours."

Kathryn opened her eyes in a look of innocence. "Why, 'Manda, I don't know what you mean."

"Oh, yes, you do," her aunt returned grimly.

Kathryn laughed and kissed the older woman on the cheek before joining her uncle on the verandah. The men were deep in discussion, but Mitchell looked up briefly as she slipped gracefully into one of the comfortable wicker chairs. When he smiled at her, Kathryn felt her pulse rate increase.

She was now close enough to notice small imperfections in the handsome face. There were smile creases at the corners of his eyes, and under his tan she could see a scattering of almost invisible freckles. He threw back his head, laughing at something Nate said, and an unexpected thrill rippled through her. Kathryn looked away from him in an effort to distract herself.

The view from the verandah was tranquil, and she relaxed a little, contemplating the familiar scene. The afternoon breeze barely ruffled wide fields laden with ripening feed crops that would provide much of the fodder for the dairy herd during the coming winter.

Stands of trees added contrasting hues of darker green, though the leaves were beginning to be touched with the gold of late summer. In the far distance, the shadowy outlines of Vermont's famous Green Mountains could be seen, a constant backdrop of beauty that Kathryn felt she would never tire of enjoying.

Nate called her back. "Kathryn . . ." He paused until he was sure he had her attention. "I'd like you to consider a proposition Mitch has for you. He wants you to come to work for him in Boston."

Casting a swift sideways glance at their visitor, Kathryn felt sure his unusual impassivity indicated a lack of enthusiasm for the "proposition." "Why, Nate, are you trying to get rid of me again?" she asked lightly. Lowering her voice confidentially, she addressed Mitchell. "He's been after me to get another job, as far away as possible, ever since I started here two years ago. Do you think he's trying to tell me something?"

"Now, Kathryn," her uncle protested, hurt. "You're the finest help I could have! Don't I leave you in complete charge when I'm gone? You practically run the place with that computer of yours. But you're wasted here. You need more training than I can give you, and you need to see more of the world. Take Mitch out to see your setup, and then he'll tell you what we have in mind."

Nate lifted his strong frame from the wicker chair.

"Listen to Mitch, honey. It's a chance that might never come your way again. And it's the chances we don't take that we most regret." One large finger caressed the side of Kathryn's soft cheek as if to persuade mutely where words might fail. With one significant look at Mitchell, the burly dairyman was gone, the door swinging behind him.

Mitchell spoke at last. "Well, Kathryn?"

She felt wary, pinned to the chair by his cool gaze. "Maybe you'd better tell me about this job you two have cooked up for me."

"Your uncle believes you have a real flair for dealing with computer systems." Clearly he was politely refraining from voicing his own doubts on the matter. "I might be able to find a place for you in my organization."

Handling files from A to B somewhere in the supply room, no doubt, Kathryn thought. Before telling him what she thought of the idea of uprooting herself from a situation where she was perfectly content to toddle off to the doubtful pleasure of a "place" in his organization, she decided to have some fun with him. She owed him something for that little scene in the barn.

"What kind of salary did you have in mind, Mr. Grant?" she asked.

"I'm sure we can match whatever your uncle is paying."

In the spirit of the game she was playing, Kathryn named a figure about double what Nate was paying. After all, he also provided room and board, didn't he?

Mitchell's eyes widened, then narrowed. "You set a high value on yourself, Miss Lambert."

"Do call me Kathryn," she replied, batting her eyes at him.

"You know, you shouldn't let yourself be talked into something you don't really want. Nate has a fixed notion you need to get out into a bigger pond, but there's a lot to be said for little ponds."

Kathryn was hard put to keep a respectful expression on her face. Small chance he would settle for any little pond. "I can understand Nate's part in this proposition, but not yours. You can't want an amateur running around loose in your company."

He smiled audaciously. "I owe Nate."

"Well, you don't owe me." Tired of her game, Kathryn got to her feet. "Come on. I'll show you our system."

In the tiny office that held her compact electronic equipment, Kathryn found she didn't wish to reveal how much of the actual programming she was responsible for. Mitchell was sure to think she was boasting. His experience was far greater and more varied, and she didn't want to give him a chance to bestow that condescending look again.

He placed a casual hand on her shoulder as he leaned over to read the screen where she had called up one of the programs. Kathryn caught her breath. The scent of him was in her nostrils: the faintest remaining traces of his morning's splash of cologne, a breath of the coffee from lunch, and something else, warm, slightly acrid . . . and very masculine. The combination was amazingly potent.

Her fingers slipped on the keyboard and gave a wrong command to the computer. With a low laugh, Mitchell reached around her with both arms and placed his own fingers on the keys. He quickly corrected the error and gave the proper command.

It could have been Sanskrit on the screen for all Kathryn cared. She had to get out of this close contact as fast as she could before she made an absolute fool of herself! Carefully turning her head, she froze as her eyes focused on the firm curves of his mouth a scant inch away from her own.

"Wouldn't you like to sit at the keyboard and check out the system?" Her voice actually squeaked on the last word, and she inwardly castigated herself.

The deep voice held a tremor of laughter. "You're doing fine."

"I insist," she said, firmly this time. She contorted her

body and slid out of his arms, but since he didn't cooperate by stepping back, almost every inch of her came in contact with him before she was free.

He gave her an innocent smile. "You don't have much room in here, do you?"

"No, well, it's usually just me in here." Pulling herself together, Kathryn managed a bright smile. "Why don't you have a look at these print-outs?" She picked up a stack of papers and thrust them at him. "I'll be back in a minute. There's something I want to ask Nate."

Still smiling, she slipped out the door, pausing to take a restorative breath after she had shut it behind her. The smile was replaced by a frown as she set out to corner her uncle.

"Now, Kathryn, don't go getting upset," Nate urged after listening to her protests. "I did it for your own good. You think I want to see you end up like your sister?"

"There's nothing wrong with Margaret."

"She's wasted on that husband of hers, and you know it."

"Jack isn't so bad." Kathryn was on shaky ground. "So he's a little dull, and I grant you he has no sense of humor, but he's a good father, and you can't fault his farming."

"'Manda and I had to stand by and watch your folks talk Margaret into marrying when she was just a kid out of high school. They'd have done the same with you if we hadn't persuaded them to let you go to college. But they're pressuring you now, aren't they? Won't be satisfied 'til you're safely set up in the same kind of life they've always known."

"My folks love me!"

"Sure they do. But they can't see that you're different. You've got a lot to offer the right man, if you want to marry. Don't throw it away on someone like Tom Wells."

For the first time since she'd returned home from college, Kathryn considered whether Nate might be right about Margaret and herself. Margaret might have asked more of life if she'd gone off to college and seen that there was a wider world to be explored. And even if her sister was content to settle down with a stolid farmer, was that enough for Kathryn?

"Aren't you afraid I might get into mischief in Boston, Uncle Nate?" she asked curiously, her mind half on the very unstolid man in the computer room.

"I know you could get hurt, and I'd hate that, but I'd rather you took the risks than never had a chance at the prizes, honey," Nate replied candidly. "I've always found life was the richer for the risks I've taken. We're a lot alike, you and me. That's why I know you'll never be happy living the same life your folks do."

"You've been a Vermonter all your life, too, Nate."

"And always will be. It's grained pretty deep in me. When I get restless, I go. Then I'm content to come back. You haven't seen enough to make your choice. Think about it."

Kathryn recognized the ring of Vermont granite in his voice. Far more progressive than her own conventional parents, Nate still had all the obduracy and plain stubbornness of the deepest-dyed Vermonter. He wanted more for her than she was going to have if she stayed where she was. She slipped an arm around his waist and hugged him. "Okay, Nate. I'll think about it. But we'd better get back to your guest before he learns more than we want him to know about the business."

During the afternoon Kathryn did think about what Nate had said. It was asking a lot of her, though, to leave her cozy situation for the unknown world of Boston. She didn't have to marry Tom Wells if she stayed in Vermont. But in Boston she'd have to face the disturbing Mitchell Grant, with his mocking attitude toward the "farmer's daughter." He wasn't the least patronizing toward her uncle or aunt, but there was always an amused glint in his eyes when they fell on her. Kathryn felt sure he was convinced she'd never make the move from the dairy farm.

It was also pretty clear he wanted to nail down her refusal without losing Nate's regard. She wasn't surprised when Mitchell maneuvered her into being the one to see him off—alone. She stood stiffly beside the open window of his sleek gray Mercedes as he started the motor.

"About that job offer, Kathryn." The smooth, deep voice sent a tingle down her spine, as no doubt it was meant to do. "I want you to know you don't have to worry about it. I expect Nate will come around to see you're happier where you are."

He paused, and a devilish sparkle lit his green eyes. "In a way it's a pity. I have a feeling I'm going to regret not having the opportunity to do more note-comparing with you. For a novice, you do have a lot to offer." He treated her to his engaging grin, which was a shade too patronizing and more than a shade premature.

He had no idea that his words had just tipped the scales, but not in the direction he expected. Mitchell Grant needed to be taught not to make assumptions so readily. The angelic expression her aunt so deplored as evidence of mischief afoot erased the tiny frown that had begun to crease her brow.

"But you don't have to! Regret it, I mean," Kathryn heard herself saying. "If we're going to be working together, there'll be lots of opportunities."

The grin faded. "You mean you want the job?"

"I've decided I shouldn't pass up such an opportunity, since you've been good enough to offer it," she said earnestly. "I mean, it's not every day someone like me gets a chance at the big leagues. Probably Nate's right, and with you to guide me . . ." Her smile was bright with good will. It was all Kathryn could do to keep it in place while Mitchell frowned up at her. She could practically see him reassessing the situation.

At last he reached into an inner pocket and drew out a case from which he took a card. He handed it to her, saying abruptly, "Okay, you've got your chance, Miss Lambert. Be at this address on the twelfth. Unless you change your mind."

The purr of the powerful motor became a low growl as his foot pressed impatiently on the accelerator. His eyes conducted a lingering, head-to-toe review of the shapely form beneath the pullover and skirt, and his expression was both a challenge and a warning.

A faint flush appeared high on her cheekbones, but her guileless blue gaze didn't waver. "I don't think I'll change my mind, Mr. Grant."

Kathryn stepped back as the Mercedes pulled away with a muted roar and a spurt of gravel. She stared down the road long after it had disappeared from sight, absently fingering the card in her hand and trying to ignore the possibility that she might just have made the biggest mistake of her life.

2

~~~~~~~~~~~~~~~~~

Kathryn arrived early at the offices on Boylston Street. Mitchell would expect a farmer's daughter to be up at dawn with the cows and waiting on his doorstep, no doubt. She touched a hand to her hair, neatly braided and wrapped around her head. The casual clothes she had worn for her job with her uncle had not seemed appropriate for a Boston office job.

So she'd brought with her an assortment of preppie clothes from college until she could figure out what people wore here. Fortunately, her taste had always run to classic styles. The burgundy twill skirt and the Oxford cloth shirt she was wearing couldn't possibly be out of place.

The offices were not yet unlocked, and she was forced to stand in the doorway, watching the crowds surge along the street. Long before he reached her side she was able to pick Mitchell out of the passersby. For one thing, he was the only person she recognized. For another, he stood out in a crowd, not necessarily because of his height or even his handsome face, but because of his bearing. You had only to look at him to see that he was self-confident, assured that he was going places.

"You're early," he muttered as he came abreast of her, his key already poised for the lock. "There's no need to get here before anyone else. You don't get extra points for it."

"I'm an early riser," she explained, her eyes wide with innocence. "You have to be on the farm, you know."

"I'm sure." He flung the door open rather aggressively and stepped back for her to enter in front of him. They were in an impressively modern lobby, small but outfitted with leather sofas and a handsome oak reception desk. "My secretary will give you a key."

"That would be nice." Kathryn took in every detail of the room, allowing her gaze to encompass the computer on the desk, the elevator against the back wall and the prints that adorned the lobby. "Where will I work?"

The question seemed to catch him off guard. He dumped the pile of envelopes he'd picked up onto the receptionist's desk and turned to meet her interested gaze. "That will depend on a number of things. Come into my office and we'll discuss your job."

He led her past a conference room to an enormous office at the back. Kathryn liked the wood, leather, and brass that warmed the modern decor. Mitchell motioned impatiently toward the comfortable leather chair that faced his desk and waited until she'd seated herself. Her eager, expectant face seemed to irritate him, and he frowned at her, remaining standing so that he towered over her.

"Your uncle assured me you have a certain familiarity with computers. We'll need to test that knowledge in order to find the precise spot into which you'll best fit." His eyes ran over her tall, slender form as she sat with her hands folded obediently in her lap. There was a measuring look in his eyes that had nothing to do with her qualifications as an employee. His gaze lingered too long on her slim, nylon-clad legs. When he raised his eyes, he encountered her exasperating look of earnest interest.

"We develop computer software at Technology Plus," he informed her as he eased himself into his chair and swung one leg negligently over the other. "What we need to find out is your level of expertise. If you're just another keypunch operator, I can find you a job with a larger, more appropriate company."

"I've done more than that," she protested. "I've written programs for Uncle Nate's system to keep track of the manure and stuff."

"Oh?" he said skeptically. "How many languages do you know?"

Kathryn cocked her head at him in such a way that it was impossible for him to see the twinkle in her eyes. "Well, French and a smattering of Spanish. I don't see how either of them would be very useful to you."

His fingers drummed loudly on the arm of his swivel chair. "I wasn't talking about foreign languages, Kathryn. Computer languages: COBOL, FORTRAN, BASIC. Surely you've heard of one of them."

"Yes," she agreed, enthusiastic. "BASIC. That's what I used for the manure program. That's the only one I know. And, actually, I had a little help with it."

"I can imagine," he sighed, shifting in his seat so that he seemed to lean clear across the desk toward her. "Most of my employees are technical people, Kathryn. They have a great deal of experience and expertise in what they do. They're applications programmers and systems programmers. We have two marketing people and a few clerical people. And we have three project leaders who supervise the three programming teams. What I'm going to do is assign you to one of them."

"Oh, that would be wonderful, Mr. Grant." She beamed at him, a smile so bright it made her eyes seem to glow, a phenomenon that those closest to Kathryn would have recognized immediately. Her new employer had no way of knowing that this was a sure sign that her puckish sense of humor was in play.

He hesitated, distracted. "It's not necessary to call me Mr. Grant. Around here we call each other by our first names. You may recall that mine is Mitchell."

"Certainly I remember. We had a bull named Mitchell once."

He stared at her for a long moment before pressing a finger to the intercom button. Without glancing away from her, he raised the phone and said, "Susan, would you come in here a moment?"

If he was trying to discomfort Kathryn with his lengthy stare, he didn't quite succeed. He did manage to make her aware of the firmness of his jaw line, and the intensity of his green eyes. She felt a nervous flutter somewhere in the region on her stomach and sternly refused to glance away from him. It was hard to maintain her look of wide-eyed innocence under the onslaught of that speculative stare, but she reminded herself of his impossible behavior at the farm, and his far from flattering assumption of her intelligence right here in the office, and she managed at least not to fidget.

An attractive blond woman entered the office. Kathryn guessed her to be approximately her own age. Mitchell smiled at the woman and introduced her as Susan Braun. "This is Kathryn Lambert, our newest employee. I'm assigning her to Jim Zachary's team; possibly he can find something for her to do." He sounded as though he sincerely doubted it. "I want you to help her get settled in."

Mitchell then turned to Kathryn and asked abruptly, "Where are you staying?"

"Temporarily, at the Diamond Residence Club on Exeter Street."

"Do you know enough about Boston to find an apartment?" He didn't wait for her to reply before continuing to Susan, "No, you'd better give her some advice. She'll just end up somewhere wretchedly inappropriate if you don't, and I'm responsible to her uncle."

"Okay," Susan said. "I'll help her find something. Do you want me to take her to Jim Zachary now?"

"If you would." He returned his attention to Kathryn. "I'll be out of town for a few days. Between them, Susan and Jim should be able to keep you busy. Just don't get in the way. Jim's working on an important project, and I don't want it held up because he has to coddle you. Is that clear?"

"Very." Kathryn could feel her temper rising, so she kept her eyes lowered to her hands. "I'm very good at keeping busy."

"I'm sure you are," he said smoothly. "Now, if you'll excuse me, I have a few things to finish before I catch my plane."

Kathryn followed Susan out of the room without glancing at her new employer. In the lobby, however, she met Susan's puzzled expression. "Is he always like that?" she asked, keeping her tone light.

The other woman frowned and shook her head. "Almost never. For a high-powered entrepreneur, he's very easygoing. He's more likely to use charm than . . . well, whatever it was he was using." She seemed embarrassed.

Kathryn grinned. "Condescension? He found me on a dairy farm and employed me against his better instincts. Don't worry about it. I'm sure everything will work out all right."

"Well, I hope so," Susan said dubiously. "I'll take you to meet Jim Zachary."

Upstairs, they wound their way through a labyrinth of desks and cubicles. There seemed to be a computer on every available surface. Susan explained that Technology Plus had fifteen employees, including Mitchell and now herself. "It's more elegant downstairs where marketing is," she said. "Both our sales people are in the field this week. The technical people are on this floor. Jim's back this way. He has three programmers and technicians working with him, but they seem to be a little short-handed. I do data entry for them when things aren't too busy in the front office."

Jim Zachary was sitting at a cluttered desk, poring over a computer print-out. His straight, sandy hair fell forward onto the rims of his glasses, and his lips were pursed in a soundless whistle. He wore a faded plaid shirt and jeans, with scruffy tennis shoes. It took two attempts for Susan to get his attention.

"Mmmm?" he murmured, turning preoccupied eyes on the two women. "Oh, Susan. Did I send for you?"

Susan shared an amused glance with Kathryn. "They're all like that, more or less. You get used to it." She returned her gaze to Jim and said, "No, you didn't send for me. I want you to meet Kathryn Lambert. Mitch has hired her to give you a hand."

Jim started to acknowledge the introduction when he abruptly remembered that it might be more polite for him to rise to his feet. Once there, his lanky body looked almost storklike, the shoulders slumped slightly forward. He extended his right hand with a movement so swift that Kathryn nearly stepped backward in her surprise. His grip was painfully firm.

"Terrific," he proclaimed. "We could use some help. Have you worked on any security systems before, Kathryn?"

"Oh, no. I don't think Mr. Grant had anything like that in mind for me. I've written a few programs for my uncle's farming business—farm profit analysis, depreciation schedules—nothing more complex than that."

Jim's face fell. "Too bad. We could use someone with more experience."

"I learn quickly," Kathryn hastened to assure him. She hadn't seen anyone look so disappointed in ages. "There are bound to be things I can do—data entry, running equipment, that sort of thing—that would give your team more time to work on the technical problems."

"I suppose so." Jim looked as if she were speaking Greek to him, and he turned to Susan for an explanation. "Does she mean the kind of thing you do for us?"

"Um, yes, I guess so. But she knows a lot more than I do about computers, Jim, so she'll be able to help more."

Kathryn wasn't at all sure she knew more about computers than Susan did, but she was loath to say so until absolutely necessary. It seemed a great pity to disillusion the poor man further, especially now as he tried to conjure up a smile for her in an effort to make amends for his possibly rude behavior.

"Welcome aboard," he said heartily. "I'm sure you'll find some things to do. Look around . . ." His voice drifted off into silence, and he stood awkwardly rubbing his palms together, his gaze surreptitiously already back on the print-outs on his desk.

Susan stepped into the breach. "I still have to show her around the office and explain our procedures to her, Jim. Later I'll give her the data you left on my desk Friday to enter, and we'll get her started that way. The only cubicle we have available right now is the one beside Ruth, so you'll find Kathryn there when you need her."

"Sure, sure. That's great," he mumbled as he sprinted back to his chair.

Kathryn could tell it was going to be a long day.

The search for suitable—(and inexpensive)—accommodations took the better part of a week. The small apartment she found on Anderson Street had three rooms, if you counted the tiny area described in the ad as a kitchen. The furnishings were a bit worn, hardly enough for even a pretense to gracious living, but they suited Kathryn's minimal requirements. The building was certainly a great deal better than the crumbling Diamond Residence Club.

She moved in on Saturday and spent the remainder of the weekend cleaning and adding necessary items to cheer up the place with a little color. While she worked, she considered what she could do about her job. On her uncle's farm she knew precisely what her duties were. No one was scrambling around trying to find things for her to do. Her uncle had never underestimated her intelligence the way Mitchell did, treating her like some hick from the cow pastures of Vermont.

If he expected a naive, accommodating rustic female, he had another think coming! But Kathryn wasn't averse to putting him on a little.

With her arms deep in a drawer of the somewhat dilapidated bureau in the bedroom, she paused, feeling a qualm as she considered that her own behavior wouldn't bear close scrutiny either, if she were perfectly honest about it. Then she shrugged and resumed arranging her clothing in the drawer. She knew all about men of his type, didn't she? Barry had certainly taught her it didn't pay to worry about the feelings of men who thought more highly of themselves and their ambitious goals than of mere ordinary people like herself.

Young, unused to the freer ways of college men, and eager for the wonder of love, she had been vulnerable to Barry's easy charm and sophisticated ways. It had taken her a while to see the basic ruthlessness that lay beneath the surface. A wry grin twisted her lips. Besides that, he'd too frequently greeted her impish sense of humor with a blank look. So few people could appreciate her enjoyment of life's amusing side.

Well, she'd learned with Barry that it wasn't smart to get seriously involved with that type of man. She could ignore the flutter of excitement she'd felt in Mitchell's office that morning if she remembered the potential consequences. Her most important task now was to prove to her new employer that she could fill a spot in his organization, not some more personal role.

By the time she left for work Monday morning, she had settled on what she could do. Her first week had been spent becoming familiar with what was going on at Technology Plus and finding useful things to do, but she'd begun to see certain possibilities. There was a comment of Jim's that kept running through her mind: "We'd get a hell of a lot more work done around here if someone would organize the place a little."

Technology Plus was a conglomeration of individuals, most of them computer geniuses of one sort or another. Unfortunately, geniuses aren't often concerned with the organization of their resources. Kathryn had spent a number of wasted hours just locating the information she needed to complete various assignments, so she understood Jim's comment. What Technology Plus needed was a system set up to control the use of the organization's resource files. Even the marketing data, so necessary to determining a customer's needs against the company's products, was not in particularly accessible form.

When she arrived early, as she always did, she went straight to her desk and began to draft an outline of her possible duties. These bore some resemblance to a job description, as opposed to Mitchell's careless instructions to help out where she could. It now seemed imperative that she have a job description if she was going to stay. And she *was* going to stay, because she'd gotten herself an apartment, and she was going to prove to her employer that even a farm girl could handle a little data-base management!

Kathryn looked up when she heard footfalls approaching her desk. In the week since he'd been gone, she'd almost forgotten how attractive Mitchell was. She swallowed, her mouth a little dry, as he sauntered toward her looking devastatingly handsome in a linen jacket the color of ripe wheat. He stopped at her desk and leaned against it casually, his hands in the pockets of his brown slacks. He was all virile male as he smiled down at her. Kathryn firmly repressed the quick response she felt and managed a bright smile. "Welcome back, Mitchell."

"You look well settled in," he remarked, looking at her rather than the work stacked on her desk.

In spite of her resolve not to let him affect her, Kathryn couldn't help feeling glad she'd bought her new dress. The pale blue, feather-light challis print made her look as fresh and cool as it was possible for a redhead to appear. She had caught up her fiery tresses into one thick braid, looped high on her head, but already the humidity had caused damp tendrils to escape, forming a bright nimbus around her piquant face. Mitchell's glance lingered and traveled, showing her his male appreciation of the way the dress discreetly showed off her slender waist and the feminine curves above and below. She watched him warily.

"I like what you've done with your braids." His lean fingers reached out and lightly touched the looped coil. His hand fell away, caressing a stray tendril in passing, brushing lightly against the side of her cheek. His eyes fell to the partially open drawer that held a few of her personal items.

She pushed the drawer closed. "Yes, I've found a few things I can do here."

"Such as?"

There was amusement underlining the skeptical lift of his brows. Ignoring it, she ticked off the various activities she'd engaged in during her first five days with the company. "And I've just worked up this job description," she concluded, extending it toward him.

He skimmed it rapidly, then reread the sheet. "This is data-base management," he said with surprise.

"Yes."

"We're a small firm, Kathryn."

"Small and disorganized," she retorted. "There are too many things that can't be retrieved without wasted effort. It would just be like setting up a filing system and maintaining it, only on computer. You need to have easier access to certain resources, and so will your marketing people. It's something I could do that would justify the salary you're paying me," she added with a puckish grin.

Mitchell didn't answer right away. He was watching the tempting little quiver at the corner of her mouth. Reaching up to adjust the knot of his tie, he cleared his throat. "Yes, well, I'm sure it would be useful, but I doubt if you have the knowledge to put it into practice yet. We can't spare the time it would take someone to show you all the ins and outs of the systems."

"If there's one thing I learned on the farm, it was that training people is almost always cost effective. Jim has already shown me enough to make the project feasible; otherwise I wouldn't have suggested it."

"What have I shown you?" Jim asked curiously, sticking his head around the corner of her cubicle.

Mitchell thrust the job description at him. "Kathryn seems to think she can handle this."

Jim pushed his glasses farther up on his nose and quickly read the single sheet of paper before glancing from one to the other. "Sure she can," he agreed off-handedly. "And it's just the sort of thing we need around here. I'll tell you something, Mitch. I was a little surprised when you sent her to me with no experience and all, but she's just the ticket to shape things up at Tech Plus. We don't need any more bright programmers; we need a little organization."

While the stunned look was still on Mitchell's face, Jim gave a brief nod and disappeared back into his office. Kathryn had modestly lowered her eyes and was surprised when the job description was thumped down on her desk with no ceremony. "All right," he grunted. "You can give it a try. No one else around here would be interested in doing it."

"I'm so glad you're pleased," she murmured, not looking up.

Mitchell ignored her sarcasm. Perhaps he didn't recognize it. "Did you find a place to live?" he asked.

"Oh, yes. I moved in over the weekend. It's on Anderson Street."

"Could have been worse," he muttered as he turned

away. "Don't forget to leave the address with Susan for her employee files."

"I've already put it on her desk."

With Mitchell back in the big office downstairs, the entire building seemed to undergo a subtle change. Though the employees generally worked hard, their conscientiousness increased when there was any likelihood that their boss would appear from the elevator or, more frequently, the stairway, taking two or three steps at a time. Kathryn thought he passed through their midst like a cruising predator that had eaten but was not averse to checking out his next meal.

She learned not to jump or fumble with the controls of her keyboard when he unexpectedly appeared on her horizon, raking her with his comprehensive gaze, looking down his nose at her with that speculative, condescending expression—or what was worse, a preoccupied glance changing to one of amused pessimism when he saw the stacks of work piled around her station.

It only hardened her resolve to make something of her job, to demonstrate once and for all that he was not as good a judge of a person's abilities as he thought. He seemed to have forgotten any inclination to follow up on a more personal interest.

By Thursday, Kathryn felt she had gotten a good start on her new duties and was feeling particularly cheerful when she returned to her apartment. It felt good to shower in the tiny bathroom and slip into her green halter top and shorts. The late summer evening was hot and muggy.

Since her hair took so long to dry, she opted for maximum coolness and let it hang in one long braid down her back. Still damp, the braid was a long lick of dark flame against the green top. Like most redheads, she didn't tan easily, and with her white skin and eyes that were almost cobalt in their blueness, she could look quite flamboyant if she chose. Most of the time she chose to play down her striking coloring.

She hummed as she went about preparing her dinner and ate it comfortably curled up in a chair in the living room. While she ate, she read a novel she'd started the previous evening, becoming so engrossed in it that she simply shoved her dishes onto a small table beside her when she was finished.

The sharp peal of her doorbell startled her, and she glanced at her watch. Nine o'clock already, and she certainly wasn't expecting anyone. Boston wasn't Vermont, where neighbors dropped in on the spur of the moment. Some very dangerous person might be out there, and she hadn't thought to put the chain on the door when she came in. As a precaution, she tiptoed over and slipped it on now before calling out, "Who's there?"

"Mitchell Grant."

Kathryn didn't like the way her heart sped up at this announcement. She slid the chain back again and cautiously opened the door.

"You should leave the chain on while you open it," he informed her, leaning against the jamb with his arms crossed over his chest. "Then when you've seen that it really is someone you know, you can take it off again."

It was the first time she'd seen him casually dressed. The cords he wore fit his lean hips and powerful thighs closely, and his white short-sleeved shirt looked cool against the dark tan of his throat and arms. Her eyes were drawn against her will to the fine brown hair that grew thickly on his forearms and on the tanned triangle visible where his shirt collar lay open.

"I recognized your voice," she said, a trifle huskily.

This information seemed to please him, and he stepped into the room confidently with an easy smile. Since she had first opened the door, he had been studying every detail of her brief shorts and top, and now he seemed fascinated by the long thick braid, which had fallen over one shoulder.

"Why are you here, Mitchell?"

"I wanted to check the place out, so I could assure myself your uncle wouldn't be alarmed at where you're living."

"I've already written him about it. I'm sure he'd approve."

Mitchell looked around the small living room, taking in the dirty dishes and the open novel left on the over-stuffed chair. The sofa was covered with a nubby green material that made him frown. "I suppose there's more to it than this," he suggested.

"There's a kitchen and a bath and a bedroom."

When she didn't offer to show them to him, he walked past her and into the minuscule kitchen. "You couldn't turn out much in this culinary haven," he murmured.

"There's only me to cook for. I won't be doing anything fancy."

He shrugged and went along the short hall to the bath, where her few cosmetics were resting on a windowsill and her nightgown hung on the hook behind the door. He eyed the latter with some interest—a simple flower-print batiste—but made no comment. The bathroom was ancient but serviceable, a makeshift shower clinging tenuously to the wall above a large old tub. Traces of steamy dampness were still evident in the room. His nostrils flared slightly at the scent of the light bath powder she'd used.

"You should probably have your landlord look at that," he remarked, gesturing at the shower as he retreated from the room.

Kathryn had no intention of doing any such thing, but she didn't bother to tell him so. He stood in the doorway of the bedroom and surveyed the double bed and chest of drawers. They were the only pieces of furniture it contained. Kathryn intended to sew curtains for the window, which looked out on a weedy yard.

Mitchell turned away from the room abruptly, almost

colliding with Kathryn, who was standing directly behind him, feeling a mounting sense of annoyance, as well as the irrepressible excitement his presence always seemed to bring. "How about offering me a cup of coffee?" he suggested. A charming smile stretched his wide mouth, but the expression in his eyes was more disturbing.

"It's rather late."

"Nine o'clock?" He shook his head wonderingly. "Surely you don't go to bed with the chickens in Boston."

Goaded, Kathryn shrugged and headed for the kitchen. He didn't follow her, but draped his long body at one end of the nubby sofa where he could watch her through the doorway. "I thought you might need some advice on living in Boston," he called to her.

"Like what?"

He offered a few cautionary tales about young women who went out alone after dark or didn't keep their doors locked. Kathryn wondered if his warnings against strange men included bosses. She wished she hadn't put on the shorts. Those lingering glances at the office had been unnerving enough. Now the entire length of her was on view, and as he talked she was only too aware of the gleam in his eyes. Her fingers trembled slightly as she poured the coffee into a single cup and asked if he took anything in it.

"Just black." He looked surprised when she handed it to him. "Aren't you having any?"

"No, I only drink it in the morning."

When she stood undecided about where to sit, he patted a place on the sofa beside his corduroy-clad thigh. Kathryn took a seat at the other end of the sofa, only to have him grin knowingly at her. "You seem to have found a good spot . . . at the office," he said. "Jim is pleased with what you managed to do while I was away, and everyone seems to agree that your new project will be useful."

"Thank you. I'm sure I can handle it, with a little help from everyone."

"Don't—" he began, then stopped himself, letting the frown that had started to develop evaporate. Instead he moved a little closer to her, using the excuse of putting his cup on the small coffee table that was positioned in front of the sofa. "There's always a lot of confusion when you start a new job," he offered sympathetically. "Especially when it means moving to the city from a place where you've been comfortable. You must miss the farm."

Kathryn was very suspicious of his sudden empathy, and she didn't like the way one of his arms managed to stretch along the back of the sofa so that his hand was just above her shoulder. "Yes, I miss the farm," she admitted. "When you're used to country living, the city seems crowded and rushed. You walk on concrete all day instead of on dirt and grass. The air isn't fresh, and there's too much traffic."

"I feel responsible in a way for taking you from your home." His voice was compassionate, warm. "And I haven't treated you very well since you came. I'd like to make up for that."

"You don't need to—"

"I'd like us to be friends, Kathryn. There aren't many women I'd say that to, but you're rather special. For your age, you're remarkably unspoiled, and perhaps a little too beautiful to be safe on your own." His hand edged down to come to rest on her shoulder, and one fingertip softly massaged the flesh exposed by her brief halter top. "You're a warm-hearted person who needs friendship and affection to be truly happy. Besides," he finished softly, "your uncle would want me to help you adjust to life in Boston, to take a guiding hand in seeing that you enjoy yourself here." There was a question hovering in the ardent gaze he bent on her.

The combination of his touch, his nearness, and the

glowing green warmth of his eyes was having its effect. She was well aware that the caressing note that had crept into his voice was not a prelude to "friendship" but to something else altogether. This had to be stopped. She put on her best look of wide-eyed innocence. "Yes, I could use a friend."

"I could be a sort of cousin," he whispered, moving his head closer. His lips curved confidently. When they had almost reached hers, she turned her face fractionally so that he lightly grazed her cheek.

"Oh, how nice!" she exclaimed, jumping up. "That's really kind of you, Mitchell. You're the only one here who's even seen the farm and knows what it means to me." Her eyes sparkled with feigned delight. "I can talk to you about it sometimes, you know. That's something I couldn't do with any of the other people at the office."

She made her way slowly, walking backwards to the door. Reluctantly he rose and followed her. "It'll be terrific to have someone to talk to. Susan and Jim and the others are nice people, but they don't understand the way you do. Vermont is so special!"

"Kathryn—"

"How I'll miss the autumn change of color. There won't be anything like it in Boston." She managed to wrench open the door, paying particular attention to the chain. "It was so good of you to come by to see that I'm all right. I'll be sure to lock up right after you're out. Thanks for the warning."

Mitchell gave her a long, hard stare as he allowed her to maneuver him into the hallway. Kathryn could tell he was about to say something, but she quickly interjected, "See you at work tomorrow," before neatly closing the door in his face. She leaned against it for a moment, stifling a giggle, and then twisted the deadbolt and put on the chain. The sound of his footsteps gradually died away in the hall outside.

Kathryn picked up his barely touched cup of coffee and carried it to the kitchen sink. As she watched the last of the dark liquid swirl down the drain, she muttered, "If a country girl is what you expect, Cousin Mitchell, a country girl is what you'll get. But she won't be a kissing cousin!"

3

Kathryn opened the drapes on Friday morning to find raindrops streaking her windowpane. She had always loved summer showers in Vermont because of the way they changed the colors in the landscape and the smell of the earth. But she knew that in the city rain only changed the traffic from slow to hopeless. She would have to leave for work earlier than usual.

Still sleepy but trying to hurry, she managed to get a run in her last pair of pantyhose. Then, after putting on a gray pant suit, she discovered that the matching blouse was in the laundry. "It's going to be one of those days," she muttered, donning a green print top that was, by her standards, too low-cut to be worn to the office. She buttoned the jacket all the way to the top, grabbed her raincoat, and ran for the bus.

The phone was ringing as she walked through the front door of Technology Plus. When it appeared that no one else was going to answer it, she picked it up and heard Susan's harried voice. "Kathryn! Thank heaven you answered. Listen, I overslept and it'll take me half an hour to get there. Can you cover for me?"

"Sure, Susan." The prospect of being Mitchell's secretary even for thirty minutes did not appeal to her, but she said, "Take your time." Obviously Mitchell wasn't in yet, or he'd have answered the phone himself. Kathryn put down the receiver and draped her dripping coat over a coatrack in the corner. The front door opened, and she turned her head in anticipation, but the man who stood there wasn't tall enough to be her employer.

This was a stranger, someone who smiled at her in what she considered an overly friendly manner. Before she could ask his identity, he started talking.

"Well, don't tell me the irreplaceable Susan has been replaced. Hi, I'm Roger Owens." He paused slightly, but Kathryn didn't offer her name. Undaunted, he continued. "I wonder what else happened around here while I was on vacation."

Under his expensive raincoat, she could see a pale lavender shirt and a coordinated tie. Kathryn took an instant dislike to him. No doubt he was one of the two salesmen she had yet to meet. She was relieved when the door opened again and Jim walked through in his yellow slicker and tennis shoes.

"Hi, Roger," he said. "How was Tahiti?"

"Fantastic."

"Did you do any sailing?"

"Oh, yeah, I did a lot of sailing."

Kathryn disliked the sly smile that accompanied this remark, and Jim waved it away with a gesture of annoyance or embarrassment before turning to her. "Susan out today?"

"No, she'll be here. I'll be with you when she gets in."

Roger watched Jim nod and walk away, then removed his raincoat. But he didn't move away from the reception desk. "So you're working with Jim on the new software?"

"Sort of." Kathryn shrugged. It was difficult to be pleasant to him, even if he was a company employee.

"One of the graphics programs? Is that your specialty?"

"No, it's the data security program, and I'm really only coordinating resources for him and for the other teams and you marketing people."

"Security?" He took a step closer. "I thought that program was already packaged and ready for distribution."

"Maybe it's a different program. This one hasn't even been alpha tested yet."

He cocked his head. "Sounds to me like Jim's off on another one of his wild goose chases. Does he have a better approach than encryption, and will it cost less? I don't believe it."

Kathryn sprang to Jim's defense. "You should. The results he's getting are terrific. Nobody's been able to crack the system, and every one of the hotshots has had a try at it."

Before Roger could reply, the elevator doors opened and Mitchell stepped out, dressed in one of his tailored lightweight business suits. There was a tiny nick on his chin, as though he had just finished shaving. A slight frown formed between his brows when he saw the two of them at Susan's desk. "Well, Roger, I see you've managed to meet Miss Lambert," he said with elaborate casualness. "Morning, Kathryn. Where's Susan?"

"She's on her way." Kathryn gave him her brightest smile, knowing it was impossible for him to comment on the previous evening's encounter with Roger standing there.

Mitchell scrutinized her face and her smile as sweet as Vermont maple syrup, then turned on his heel. "Come on in my office, Rog," he said over his shoulder.

Kathryn made sure neither man saw her smile give way to a mischievous grin. She was finding it took a lot of concentration to maintain the disguise of a bucolic maiden. It was like playing a part in a movie or a soap opera, only she had to improvise her lines each time. And she couldn't always tell when she was going to be "on camera." But it was worth the effort to see the look on Mitchell's face, especially last night on the nubby green sofa. At this rate, she was going to be able to get away with her act indefinitely.

Susan eventually arrived, her umbrella dripping, and tilted her head toward Mitchell's office. "Is he mad at me for being late?"

"I don't think so. He went right into his office with Roger Owens."

"I didn't know Roger had an appointment with Mitchell this morning," Susan remarked as she hung her coat on the rack. "He takes the most incredible vacations. This time it was Tahiti."

Kathryn was too interested in something else that had aroused her curiosity to consider it odd that an employee needed an "appointment" with his boss. "Susan, there's something peculiar around here. I'm sure there wasn't anyone else in the office when I came in. But Mitchell just came down in the elevator, and it looks like he just this minute shaved."

Susan laughed, busy settling in at her desk. "Hasn't anyone told you Mitchell has the penthouse suite?"

"You mean he lives here?"

"Mm-hm. I wouldn't like it myself, but it seems to suit Mitch. He lives and breathes his business, so why not sleep with it as well?" Her face broke out in a grin. "Right after I came to work here, he invited my husband and me over for dinner. He has the place fixed up really neat. But what he did was get us talking about our plans for the future, and he had it out of us in no time that we weren't planning on a family any time soon."

She shook her head. "Which meant it would be worthwhile training me, you see. If he weren't so smooth about it, he'd probably get a poke in the nose."

Susan's words made Kathryn very thoughtful as she headed for the floor above and her own cubicle. Her estimation of Mitchell's character had obviously been quite accurate. It would be worth her while to be wary of him. And, if she was lucky, to keep a step ahead of him.

At eleven Susan buzzed her on the intercom and told her Mitchell wanted to see her in his office. Kathryn was instantly alert. Was this to be another round in the match between the milkmaid and the city slicker? Or was it solely business? She was prepared to defend her new duties to the death. Or at least until she was hoarse.

The morning had turned warm and muggy, but Kathryn didn't want to present herself in his office in the low-cut green blouse, so she slipped on her jacket and buttoned it all the way up. As she walked to the elevator, she tucked a yellow pad under her arm. Better not to give him anything to object to.

When she paused in the open doorway of his office, Mitchell waved her in. He was standing by a chalkboard, chalk in hand, making adjustments to the notes and numbers he had scrawled in his bold handwriting. "Have a seat," he said absently before moving to his desk to punch information into the computer terminal. Almost to himself he muttered, "These figures look really good."

"What figures?" she asked, sliding onto the leather chair.

He was back at the board, adding more data. "Sales forecasts. I just talked with the marketing people we use in Chicago and Los Angeles. We're planning the marketing strategy for the security program."

His jacket was off, and Kathryn found herself staring at the trim hips outlined by his well-cut slacks. Her brother-in-law Jack was hippy, and she had always found it terribly unappealing. Of course, Jack didn't own any tailored slacks.

"Here's a job for you," he said, immediately starting to rattle off information.

Kathryn took notes rapidly on the yellow pad, agreeably surprised that he was trusting her with an important task. She didn't bother to tell him he was talking too fast. Fifteen minutes later he finally paused to ask, "How soon can you have something ready for me to look at?"

"It would take two or three days of steady work, but if I continue helping Jim—"

"Forget Jim for now," he cut in. "Stay with this project. We're going to pour a lot of money into marketing this product, and we need accurate data to work with. Come to me for help if you hit any snags. This has top priority."

Kathryn felt slightly off balance with this sudden change in his attitude toward her. He was actually treating her like a member of the team. But it would mean working closely with him, at least for the next few days. Was that going to complicate her game? She started to get up, but Mitchell had flung himself into his chair and was smiling expansively at her.

"Well," he said, "it looks like it wasn't such a bad idea to transplant the Flower of Vermont into the alien soil of Boston."

She pasted a demure smile on her face and said, "Uncle Nate will be real happy to hear that."

His eyes narrowed for a moment, then he grinned. "You're going to be a wilted flower if you wear jackets like that on days like this, Kathryn."

"My blouse is a bit . . . immodest."

"I don't mind." The grin had broadened. "As long as you don't go around like Shirley."

"Who's Shirley?"

"She used to work here. A bright programmer, but some of the outfits she wore . . ." He shook his head. "The guys had a pool going, trying to guess the date when the plunge in her neckline would meet the slit in her skirt. But she left before the big day came around." He eyed her jacket once again. "The humidity's eighty-seven percent right now, Kathryn."

She *was* uncomfortably warm. Well, she'd have a little

fun with him, then make a fast retreat. "I suppose there are times when one has to make allowances." She reached up and slowly unbuttoned just one button at her throat.

"That's not much of an allowance. You look like some Victorian lady applying for a job."

Kathryn made a show of reluctantly undoing one more button. There was no trace of the low-cut green blouse in sight. She'd have to get down to the fourth button before the fabric would show. "I don't mean to dress prudishly. But one has to be discreet in an office," she informed him severely.

"Not that discreet, or you'll collapse from heat prostration."

She shrugged and worked slowly at the third button. His eyes were trained on her chest, and his fingers drummed softly on his desk. When the third button was released, with still no sight of the blouse, he demanded, "Do you really have something on under that jacket?"

"Well, of course I do," she retorted, indignant. Her hands dropped to her lap. "I'll be quite cool enough this way."

"I want to see it."

"I beg your pardon?"

"I want to see your blouse."

Kathryn gazed at him in mock horror. "I can't just go around taking my clothes off for anyone who asks."

"Take your jacket off, Kathryn."

She sighed. "Oh, very well. It's terribly stuffy in here, isn't it?" Her hand hesitated at the fourth button. The drumming of his fingers stopped. "After all, I wouldn't have worn the blouse if it weren't decent. I've even worn it at the farm. Well, not the farm exactly. When I went to the movies in town."

"Take your jacket off, Kathryn."

With a shrug she quickly undid the rest of the buttons and stripped off the jacket. The green linen blouse revealed only a slight bit of decolletage.

He exhaled and sat back in his chair. "You call *that* immodest?"

"Well, think of all the advice you gave me last night about women in the city." She looked down at her lap so he couldn't see the mischievous gleam in her eyes. "That was a big help to me. Uncle Nate would certainly appreciate your guidance."

She looked up to find a mixture of disbelief and shrewd appraisal in his eyes. His mouth stretched in a calculatedly charming grin, effective if suspect.

"And I'm sure he'd appreciate my taking you to lunch." His grin was now decidedly wolfish.

Kathryn regretted giving way to her impulsive button game. "That's not necessary, Mitchell."

But he was already coming around his desk, his hand sliding under her elbow. "Nonsense. I've been away, so I haven't given you the attention you deserve."

She found herself at the office door before she could object. "It's still early. I don't usually go before twelve or one."

Mitchell relieved her of the yellow pad and her jacket by tossing them on Susan's desk as he breezed past with her in tow. "Kathryn and I are going to lunch, Susan."

On the sidewalk the heat hit them at once. Mitchell guided her to the right, walking briskly along the busy street. Not a trace of the earlier rain remained.

"Are we catching a train or something?" she complained at the second intersection. Her breath was coming quickly, and a fine dew of perspiration had broken out on her upper lip.

"Sorry." He slowed and looked down at her, smiling. "I tend to move fast when I make up my mind where I'm going."

"I've noticed. I'd hate to get in your way."

His brows shot up quizzically. "You make me sound ominous. I'm not such a bad fellow." He dropped her elbow and slid his arm around her waist, maneuvering her out of the way of a group of tourists exploring the Prudential Center.

"Really?" Kathryn sounded dubious. "Well, you do seem to know your way around."

He cast her a sharp glance but said only, "I've been in Boston a long time. When you've been here awhile, you'll hardly remember what it's like back on the farm."

"That's what I'm afraid of," she muttered as they crossed Prudential Plaza and walked up a broad flight of steps into an impressive building made of large sheets of glass.

In a quietly plush restaurant high above the city streets, they were quickly seated in low, comfortable chairs. Kathryn turned to look out at the view as an attractive waitress approached their table.

"Your usual, Mr. Grant?" she asked, dimples appearing in her cheeks as she smiled.

"Right. Heineken and a reuben." He paused, considering Kathryn. "And my companion will have a glass of cold milk, won't you, my dear?"

She could tell by the twitching corners of his mouth that he was trying to rattle her in front of the amused waitress. "Yes, and a ham on rye."

When the waitress had moved off, Kathryn propped her elbows on the table and rested her chin on her crossed hands. "You never cease to amaze me, Mitchell. How do you manage to be so thoughtful?"

"I wonder myself sometimes. If you didn't want milk, you should have told her."

"I love milk." Her wide eyes blinked innocently at him. "Do you come here often?"

They chatted amicably while they waited for their food, and more sporadically as they ate. Kathryn knew he was suspicious of her country girl act, which she personally thought was as hammy as her sandwich, but he couldn't quite bring himself to believe it was a put-on.

"Why do you always wear your hair in braids?" he asked.

49

"Don't you like them?"

"They're charming. But most women would give their eyeteeth for hair that color; they wouldn't hide it under a bushel, so to speak." He studied her, as though mentally measuring. "It must be pretty long."

She nodded. "Sometimes it's a nuisance. The braids were practical for the farm."

"But you're not on the farm now."

Kathryn shrugged her shoulders slightly. "I'm comfortable with it this way."

Mitchell looked as though he intended to make some comment, but asked instead, "How about dessert?"

By the time they'd finished their lunch and walked back up Boylston, they had established a working rapport. Despite the fact that Kathryn had had to repress a lot of her natural responses to his quick wit, she was not ready to give up her game. She was too intent on finding out how long she could get away with it.

As they approached the office, he smiled down at her. "It's not so hard being friends, is it?"

His eyes were gleaming. Now she wasn't sure he wasn't putting *her* on. "I enjoyed lunch very much, thank you," she replied primly. "But I liked the walk even more, I think. Boston's so historical, you know. There are lots of things I want to see."

"Like what?" They had come to a halt just outside Technology Plus while he waited for her reply.

She wrinkled her nose at him. "Oh, the usual tourist things. I thought I'd do one of those Boston-by-foot tours. Or walk the Freedom Trail by myself."

He pretended to wince. "Wouldn't it be just as good in a Mercedes?"

"I wouldn't think so." She smiled up at him. "You can't see the inside of Paul Revere's house from a car."

"At least you can see the Boston Pops from a comfortable chair."

"Yes, I know. Susan and her husband took me a

couple of nights ago. The orchestra played some of my favorite Beatles numbers."

He looked disappointed. "Oh. Well, there are other things." He pushed the door open with the flat of his hand and ushered her inside. "Come on back in the office for a minute." He picked up the yellow pad and her jacket from Susan's desk as they passed. In his office he motioned her to sit down as he sauntered around his desk. He stood there for a moment gazing at her, his fingers toying with a small hand calculator.

"I'd like to visit you again, Kathryn. Perhaps you'll invite me over for some country cooking. Do you know how to make the dessert we had for lunch that day at the farm?"

Strange he'd remember such a small detail. "That was 'Tipsy Parson.' I know how to make it."

"Tipsy Parson?" His look told her he found this too hilarious to be true.

She couldn't help smiling back. "Really. It gets its name from the two tablespoons of sherry you pour on the sponge cake before you add the custard sauce."

"Two whole tablespoons. Wow. That's pretty hard to handle."

"Well, that's on each serving."

He laughed out loud, and his face took on a boyish quality she found disarming. Fortunately the intercom buzzed.

Mitchell pressed a button, and Susan's pleasant voice floated into the office. "It's Roger Owens. Do you want to talk to him?"

"Mmm, not right now. Tell him I'll call him later to set up a tentative luncheon appointment."

Something in the conversation struck Kathryn as not quite right. Why was Roger calling on an outside line, and why wouldn't Mitchell just stop by his office to set a luncheon appointment? In the straightforward manner most natural to her, she simply asked, "Does Roger work for Technology Plus or doesn't he?"

"No, he's a headhunter." When he saw her puzzled look, he explained. "That means he searches for the right people to fill high-level jobs in the various companies that are his clients. Roger specializes in the computer field, and he's damn good at it."

"Is Technology Plus one of his clients?"

"Yes, he's trying to find us a person to write sophisticated documentation for our software programs. Why all the questions?"

Kathryn lifted one shoulder negligently. "I just wondered how he knew so much about what's going on here if he didn't work for the company."

Mitchell became instantly alert, like an animal who sensed danger. "He doesn't know what's going on; he never gets past my office."

"He knew Jim had worked on a graphics program, and—"

"Hold it right there." Mitchell leaned across his desk, his jaw protruding. "You two must have had quite a conversation. Maybe you'd better tell me exactly what happened this morning."

Feeling apprehensive, Kathryn sat back and tried to concentrate on the scene at Susan's desk. "Roger was the first person to arrive. Then in a minute or two Jim came along."

"What did you tell Roger?" The words were uttered in a menacing tone. Their friendly rapport of just moments ago had evaporated.

"Nothing. He did all the talking. Mitchell, what's going on?"

"I'm trying to find out how much information you leaked to an outsider. You probably don't know enough to jeopardize us, but I have to be sure."

His lack of tact nettled her, but she tried to fill in the details she remembered. "He heard that I was working with Jim and asked if I knew a lot about graphics. I told him no, I was helping on the security program."

"Damn!" Mitchell slammed his hand hard on the desk top. The look on his face would have curdled milk. "That was the sixty-four million dollar question, and you answered it. He threw you the bait and you swallowed it."

"Bait? Mitchell, I don't know what you're talking about."

"It's an old trick. He deliberately fed you wrong information, hoping you'd correct him."

"But he didn't seem interested in the security program. He said Jim had a lot of crazy ideas that didn't work." Kathryn hoped this would relieve him.

Instead his mouth curled into a sardonic smile. "Oh, did he? I can hardly wait to hear what you said next."

Color rose in her cheeks, and she answered sharply. "Look, I don't know enough about the program to leak anything of value. All I said was that Jim's ideas certainly did work, and . . ." Her voice faltered. The green eyes bored into hers. "And something about the system being so good even our own people couldn't crack it." Kathryn slumped in her chair, dejected. She'd been tricked and outsmarted, made to look like the country bumpkin he took her for. "I told him the alpha testing wasn't done yet," she added in a flat tone.

"Congratulations. You did a very thorough job." There was a cold, sarcastic bite to his voice. "You let him know we're working on a secret project, what it is, who's designing it, and that it's in the early stages of development. No wonder Roger was hanging on your every word when I arrived."

"But, Mitchell, I didn't tell him any specifics about the program. And even if he broke in and stole the disks, they're all coded with—"

With a wave of his hand he cut her off. "Roger isn't that kind of criminal. He's a headhunter."

Kathryn drew a quick breath. "You mean he'd try to get Jim away from here?"

"Now you're catching on. It's a little late, but . . ." His annoyance was beginning to make his voice louder.

"Kathryn, what the hell made you think he worked here? You've been here more than a week, and you've never seen him around until this morning. Why would you go blabbing to him?"

"He arrived before opening time. He knew Susan. Jim knew he'd been on vacation in Tahiti. I thought he was one of our sales people." It was impossible not to try to defend herself. "And if Roger is a threat to your business, why didn't you warn me about him? You just turned me loose, told me to fill in where I could. You never trained me."

"That's enough! When I want a lesson in how to run my company, I won't go to an expert on milking machines." He was pacing the floor like a restless jaguar. "Do you realize that in three minutes you may have destroyed the business I've worked years to build? The team I've put together so carefully?" He stopped near her chair, and she could feel the energy pulsing through his body. "Kathryn, we were months away from the big payoff. The sales potential of this one program runs into millions of dollars, and we'd be the first on the market with it. Now that the word is out, we'll lose that edge."

Kathryn gathered her chaotic thoughts together. "But you have a solid business even without Jim's program," she protested.

He looked at her with contempt. "You don't think I plan to stay at this level, do you? It's only the first stage of my plans for Tech Plus. Before the year is out, we'll have every corporation in America with secrets to hide coming to us to help them do it. And that's just the beginning. That's what you've endangered, Miss Lambert. At that level, the 'edge' can make all the difference. What you've done is force me to alter strategy, and I don't like that."

"Surely it wouldn't help Roger to spread the word around."

He nodded absently, his mind already busy figuring angles. "Probably not. A lot depends on Jim." A frown darkened his face. "On Jim and on how much money I can get my hands on."

"Money? You mean you'd have to offer Jim more money than an outside company that Roger might find for him?"

He shook his head impatiently. "No, I need time. The important thing is to get our program on the market first, and we still have to get the bugs out of it, write the documentation . . . If I had even two more months . . . Damn! I hate being pushed into a corner like this. I hate losing control." He turned away from her and paced to the far corner of the room, his hands jammed into his pockets.

When he spoke again, his voice was low and bitter. "There's only one way to buy time. That's with a hell of a lot of money."

"Uncle Nate would help. The farm is worth a lot of money, and he's partly responsible for my being here."

"Be quiet." He gave her a withering look. "This is still my business, and I make the decisions." He strode over to the desk and picked up the phone. Kathryn noticed that he took a few deep breaths before the call went through. "Hello, John, it's Mitchell. Would you be interested in investing a little sooner in Technology Plus?"

Kathryn could hear the enthusiastic voice coming over the line, although she couldn't make out the words.

"Well," Mitchell went on in a tone that was unbelievably pleasant, "today I'm looking for money." He glanced at his watch. "I can be at your place in fifteen minutes, and we can talk about it."

All traces of good will left his face the moment he hung up. His mouth was twisted as though the conversation had left a bad taste in his mouth. It probably wasn't the right time to say anything, but she couldn't leave the office without apologizing.

"Mitchell, I'm sorry my mistake has caused so much trouble. I'll do anything I can to help set it straight."

Anger, frustration, and pride showed in his cold eyes. "I haven't forgotten that your uncle saved my life," he snapped, "but right now I'd like to wring your neck." He snatched his jacket from the brass coatrack and was out the door before the wobbling coatrack came to rest.

4

Kathryn remained slumped in the green leather chair. Why had she ever left Vermont? She could be sitting right now at her computer terminal on the farm, handling something she was competent to handle, bothering no one, gazing out over the soothing Vermont countryside. Instead she was causing a crisis in the city, out of inexperience and ignorance. She didn't know how she could face Mitchell again, the man who last night had wanted to kiss her and today wanted to wring her neck.

And Jim? Would she lose his friendship when he learned the trouble she'd caused? Susan and the others might discover, too, that she'd been the one who caused Mitchell to seek outside financing earlier than he had planned. Their loyalty to Mitch was likely to turn them against her. Only then did it occur to her that Mitch might simply fire her. How humiliating to return to the farm in disgrace!

Well, she'd get another job in Boston before she'd go home. Jim was convinced she had some skill at data-base management; even Mitch had grudgingly admitted it. There were other companies that could use her abilities. She'd graduated from a good college, where she'd often been on the dean's list. And her experience on the dairy farm counted for something. If Mitchell weren't so egotistical, he'd recognize she was more than a naive country girl.

Susan stuck her head in the doorway. "Where was Mitch going when he charged out of here like a bull?" she asked.

The image would ordinarily have struck Kathryn as being very amusing, but not now. She stood up, gathering her jacket and yellow pad. "He was late for an appointment."

"I didn't know he had one. Are you going upstairs now? Would you take something up to Howard for me?"

Kathryn grimaced. Howard was the office Lothario, and she avoided him when she could. "Sure, if I don't have to say anything to him."

Susan grinned. "Nope, just toss it on his desk."

Fortunately, Howard was away from his desk, and Kathryn was able to get back to her video display terminal. Certain files had to be set up right away in order to manipulate the data Mitchell had asked for. She worked hard, only stopping once when a fit of depression overwhelmed her—someone else might take over this job and work with Mitchell on the marketing plan. Someone who would be the recipient of his suave charm and that devastating boyish grin he bestowed on the rare occasions when he was delighted by the ridiculous.

She looked up to find Jim standing just inside her cubicle, peering at her over his glasses.

"Kathryn, did you enter the data I gave you this morning? I'm going to need to run it in about an hour."

She bit her lip. "No. I'm sorry, but Mitchell told me to drop everything and work full-time on the data base. I forgot to tell you."

"You're supposed to be working on my team."

"Well, I will be, after I've done this project for him. But I should have finished the entering first. I'll do it right now."

"No, I don't want to get you in trouble with Mitch."

"I'm already in trouble with Mitch," she said, then caught herself. "Only joking," she added brightly.

"Yeah? Funny thing to joke about."

Kathryn shrugged, but she was unable to withstand his probing look. "I made a mistake this morning. Mitchell will probably tell you about it."

"Why would he do that?"

"Because it was a pretty big mistake."

Jim pulled a chair over and sat down. "Look, I don't know about Vermont, but here in Boston we make mistakes all the time. It's no big deal. Tell me what you did wrong, and when Mitch tells me later, I'll act surprised."

His smile was too friendly to resist. Kathryn took a deep breath and said, "It happened first thing this morning. You remember I was talking with Roger Owens when you came in?" Jim nodded. "You asked him about his vacation in Tahiti, so I thought he worked here and then . . . oh, he asked me a lot of questions." Kathryn swallowed to moisten her dry throat. "Jim, I told him about your security program."

"Oh, no." Jim looked pained rather than angry. "What a dirty trick to play on you."

His sympathy only made Kathryn feel worse. "I know it doesn't do any good to say I'm sorry, but I am. I've jeopardized the success of your program, and made Mitchell go out and get an investor, and probably sicked Roger on you . . ."

"Forget about Roger," Jim said, dismissing the head-hunter with a wave of his hand that almost knocked off his glasses. "Last year he tried to get me to take a job with a big corporation. Sure, they'd pay me more money, but the work would be boring, and I'd have to wear a tie every day."

"But he might come up with an offer you can't resist."

"I doubt it. Besides, I'd rather stay with Mitchell."

"Why?"

"He's been pretty decent to me, even before I came to work for him."

Kathryn smiled her encouragement to keep him talking.

He hitched his chair a little closer. "I used to have my own business, too, only I worked out of my garage. Lots of guys started that way when the software business began to boom a few years ago. I'd written some hot programs and sales were good, but the pirates did me in."

"Pirates?"

"Yeah, some sharp operators just copied my work with a few changes, put a flashy package around it and sold it as their own. This is a very competitive business, and I'm not much of a businessman. Mitch and I used the same distributor, and we'd gotten to know each other. He tried to help me, but I didn't always listen to him. When my business finally crashed, Mitch offered me a job."

Kathryn felt like patting his hand but resisted the impulse. "Maybe you can go out on your own again sometime."

"No, I'm not really the type for it. I'd rather work on new programs and let Mitch worry about the business end of it. Wondering where your next meal is coming from tends to stifle your creativity. Mitch lets me take time off to go to conferences and workshops, and he gets me anything I need. Ever notice that chair I sit on?"

"The one without a back? I thought it came from a secondhand furniture store."

Jim grinned. "It cost four hundred dollars."

"You're kidding! That's too much to spend on a chair."

"I didn't spend it on a chair. I spent it on Jim's back."

Mitchell loomed in the doorway, eyeing the scant inches between her knees and Jim's. "That chair is designed to keep the spine in natural balance. Just the thing for a tall programmer, right, Jim?"

"It certainly got rid of my backache."

"I beg your pardon," Kathryn said stiffly. "I didn't understand."

"There are a lot of things you don't understand." Mitch sounded decidedly grumpy.

Jim shifted uneasily in his chair. "Come on, Mitch. Don't rub it in. She's feeling bad enough about what happened."

Mitch's eyes flashed a warning. "What do you know about what happened?"

"Just that Kathryn was taken in by Roger's—"

"Kathryn!" His voice made them both jump. "Don't tell me you blabbed again. Can't you understand that this is my business and I handle things my own way?"

His tone was so harsh that Jim rose and placed himself protectively between his employer and Kathryn. "Hold on a minute, Mitch. Kathryn was upset, and I wormed it out of her. She wasn't going to tell me."

Mitchell thrust his chin out and asked, "Is there some reason you're shielding Kathryn from me? Did you think I was going to take a swing at her?"

"No, but you're losing your temper, and I'm afraid you'll fire her, and I need—"

"I am not losing my temper," Mitchell said through clenched teeth. "And I'm not going to fire her. I'm going to take her off your project and reassign her to Howard's group."

"Ugh!" Kathryn interjected.

Jim frowned. "But I want her on my team! It doesn't make sense to transfer her just because—"

Mitch cut him off. "It will make sense to people who invest their money in this program. When you have a leak, you plug it."

This conjured up a distasteful image to Kathryn, but

she said nothing. Jim folded his arms across his chest and remarked, "Maybe you should transfer me, too. I walked right past Roger this morning instead of introducing him to Kathryn so she'd know he was an outsider."

Kathryn doubted that Mitchell's employees were in the habit of challenging him. His stance was aggressive, with his feet spread apart and his eyes cold. "I didn't come up here to discuss the matter. I came to arrange Kathryn's transfer."

But Jim was not intimidated. "Maybe you're going to transfer Susan, too. If she hadn't been late, Kathryn would never have met Roger."

Mitchell put up a warning hand. "That's enough, Jim."

"And if you'd been on time, Roger would have been sitting safely in your office when Kathryn—"

"What the hell's gotten into you! *I'm* the one who has to solve the problems Kathryn caused this morning, not you."

Kathryn could have hugged Jim for the calm way he faced Mitchell's wrath.

"You shouldn't dump all the blame on Kathryn; we're all partly responsible. I'm sorry, but I feel strongly about this, Mitch. Kathryn's a hard worker, and I want to keep her on my team, after she's finished this data-base stuff for you."

Mitchell jammed his hands in his pockets. "I have someone new coming in on Monday to work with you. Her name's Rita Sweeney, and she's a crackerjack at documentation and packaging. I just worked out the final details with Roger, and he says she's the best in the business."

"Roger?" Kathryn couldn't believe her ears. "You're hiring someone through Roger at a time like this?"

Mitchell's look was searing. "When you own part of this company, Kathryn, I'll consider asking your advice on these matters."

Jim cocked his head. "I can't see how a documentation expert is going to be any help with the routine stuff Kathryn does. I thought you wanted to move this project along. Then leave Kathryn with me. When you get right down to it, Mitch, she's as necessary as my chair."

The comparison was too much for Kathryn. She ducked her head so Mitchell wouldn't see her amusement, but her shoulders shook nevertheless. Jim laid an anxious hand on her shoulder.

"Don't cry, Kathryn. It'll be all right."

"I'm not crying." The eyes that peeped up were full of unholy merriment. "I'm just so proud to be as important as a chair."

"You know what I mean," he said, his voice gruff.

Mitchell glanced between the two of them and cleared his throat. "Very well, Kathryn can stay on your project, as long as she keeps a rein on her mouth." There was a strange glint in his eyes, and she could hear the lingering hostility when he said, "I'll need the first set of marketing forecast figures this afternoon. Bring them down as soon as they're ready."

Giving her a dark look, he was gone, leaving them to stare after him.

"He's been strange lately," Jim offered in apology.

"I think he's probably been strange since birth," she rejoined. "Thanks for saving me from Howard's clutches."

Jim looked uncomfortable. "I was only making my job easier, Kathryn. And I like having you around."

She smiled at him. "Well, if I don't get to work now, he'll have another reason not to keep me around."

Jim nodded and disappeared. Since it was too late for him to get anyone else to do the work he'd given her, she finished it first, skipping her coffee break. Then she worked quickly to put together the figures for Mitch, but it was already after four when she knocked at his office door.

"Come in." He was tapping commands into the

computer and didn't look up. "Close the door. It's a signal to Susan to intercept any phone calls or visitors." He waved her into a chair and, when he'd finished what he was doing, stretched out his hand for the figures without a word.

Kathryn watched as he scanned them, but her attention wandered as he worked for a while at the computer. She was brought back sharply when he snapped, "What took you so long?"

"I beg your pardon?"

"You should have had this to me an hour ago."

"I had to finish up some work for Jim. He'd given it to me this morning, and there wasn't time to find someone else to do it."

His eyes were blazing. "I thought I told you to drop everything else for this."

"I skipped my coffee break," she said defensively.

"Such a sacrifice," he mocked. "But it had to be made for Jim, of course, because he stands so firmly behind you."

He smiled then, but the quality of his smile made her swallow nervously.

"You wouldn't be making the mistake of not taking me seriously, would you, Kathryn?"

She shook her head, wary.

"Because it would be a mistake, you know," he continued. "I'm a fairly easygoing fellow. I get along with dogs and children, and I even help old ladies across the street. But when it comes to my business, and some other things, I know what I want and I pursue it. I'm not ashamed of that. You're not on the farm now. This is my turf, and I'm the man in control here."

"I know that."

"Just because I let Jim keep you on his team doesn't mean I've given up any of that control."

Her eyes widened. "Of course not."

"And don't give me that wide-eyed innocent look. I

don't believe it." With one fluid motion he was out of his chair and moving toward her.

Kathryn, alarmed by the glint in his eyes, hastily abandoned her chair. There wasn't time to put it between them before he reached her. His hands gripped her upper arms with a firmness that held her trapped.

"Look at me, Kathryn," he demanded.

She had been trying to focus on his tie; her eyes now hesitantly lifted. The green eyes glowed with mesmerizing effect. She could feel a nervous twinge run through her. His lips were so amazingly close, his jaw set with determination. She nervously moistened her lips.

"Wrong," he whispered, lowering his head to capture her mouth.

Her lips tingled from the insistent pressure, and she felt reluctant to withdraw. His mouth was persuasive, teasing her lips into clinging against his. She could feel a response start to move through her body, and she pulled back.

Kathryn opened her eyes to find him smiling at her, the green eyes gleaming. His hands were still locked firmly on her arms. When he spoke, his voice was taunting. "Not exactly a naive milkmaid's kiss, Kathryn. But then, I didn't think it would be. Shall I show you my version of the button game?"

"I don't know what you're talking about."

But his hands had moved to her waist, where he slipped her blouse out from under her slacks. When she tried to brush him away, he grasped her hands firmly and stared straight into her eyes. "That little game you played this morning with the jacket. It's called striptease." One hand slid under the blouse to her bare skin.

Kathryn stepped backward but found herself pressed up against a table. He was immediately in front of her, one hand moving to unfasten her lowest button. "A dangerous game for an innocent country girl to play. But those blue eyes would melt steel, and it's so hard to resist them." He undid another button as she stood frozen in front of him. "It's only fair for us to play your little game together."

His hand slid under the blouse and up to cup her breast. Kathryn made a murmur of protest, but his mouth closed on hers. The sensations this dual onslaught created almost stunned her. She clutched at his back to steady herself. The fiery kiss heated her blood, robbing her of any desire to struggle. His tongue teased and intoxicated her lips until they opened to invite him in.

The kiss was like an enchantment, taking over her will, promising pleasure. She could feel the tautness of his body against hers, dominating all her senses. The caress of his hands on her breasts was as titillating as his tongue in her mouth. Her body blossomed under his touch, yearning toward him.

At some point his behavior changed subtly. The cool seductiveness of his kisses and his touch became more fevered. There was a sudden urgency to him, as though he'd lost some of his iron control, been taken over by his desire. He murmured against her lips, pressed her body tightly against his, willing them both to merge in his growing passion. Kathryn could feel the flame of his desire leap across to her own flesh.

But when he ran one hand possessively down over her slacks, the fog in her brain suddenly cleared. Her resistance, so traitorously absent, now returned. Sliding her hands up into his hair, as though to caress the thick waves, she grabbed a good handful and yanked hard. The kiss ended abruptly.

"I give up," he muttered in a pained voice as she gave an extra yank for good measure. He let go of her to dislodge her grip on his hair.

Kathryn slid out from against the table, hurriedly refastening her buttons as she moved away from him. "What a crazy way to behave," she grumbled, hoping she sounded more firm than she felt. "Someone could have walked in here in the middle of all that, and then where would you be?"

Mitchell was not repentant. "It wasn't a bad place to be. I notice you're not pretending you didn't like it."

Fighting both the desire to wipe that satisfied look off his face and an almost hysterical desire to laugh, she opted for dignified silence and an air of injured pride.

A little crease appeared in his brow, but he had regained his air of command. "There's something about you, Kathryn," he said slowly. His eyes still gleamed with unquenched ardor. He shook his head, as though to clear it. "But you're right. This is no place to be doing what we were doing."

Kathryn was amazed to hear so reasonable a statement from a man who had just started to move toward her again, that unnerving gleam in his eyes.

"It's almost five o'clock," he went on. "We'd have more privacy upstairs in my penthouse." He smiled at her indignant glare and dropped a quick kiss on the tip of her nose. "No? What a pity. I really did want to show it to you."

"I have no desire to see your penthouse," she declared wrathfully as she tucked in her blouse. "And I have no desire to be molested in your office. You're angry with me for any number of things, and it's hardly businesslike of you to try to take it out on me by . . . by making a pass."

"Such a wonderfully quaint expression." He stroked back a strand of hair that had escaped onto her forehead. "I'll try to remember how coolly professional you acted during the whole episode."

Kathryn glared at him. "And I'll try to remember not to come in here with you when the door's closed."

He studied her flushed cheeks for a long moment. "Yes, that might be best for both of us. Your red hair seems to have a decidedly arousing effect on me."

"Naturally," she sniffed. "I believe red is the color they use to enrage bulls."

A deep chuckle rumbled up from his chest. "So you're the graceful matador, luring me into the fray. When you've done me in, you'll take my ear as a trophy, no doubt, and mount it in your apartment over that stupid green sofa."

Kathryn turned abruptly and stalked to the door, where she paused to whirl around, one hand on hip. "Olé!" she cried, and ran for the waiting elevator.

5

Jim was filling a cup of coffee for Kathryn when Mitch arrived in the upstairs lounge on the following Monday. Kathryn had managed to avoid her employer at work and had not answered the phone or the door at her apartment. She was pretty sure he'd tried to call and even come by once, but she had sat quietly in the overstuffed chair and ignored the impatient ringing of her bell. There was no way to tell from the hall that her living room light was on.

Mitch paused at the doorway now, studying the two of them briefly before he strolled into the room. "I'd like a word with you, Jim," he announced, but his eyes weren't on Jim's back, which was toward him. They were searching Kathryn's face for some sign, possibly a reaction to his presence. She merely met his stare with a nod of acknowledgment. "In private," he added.

"Oh, Kathryn won't be in the way," Jim said, turning to thrust a mug toward Mitch. "She knows all about the project."

"I know." The dry remark went over Jim's head, and Mitch accepted the coffee after a moment's hesitation. "It's about our outside investor for the company."

Jim looked surprised. "But Kathryn knows all about that."

Embarrassed, she muttered, "Look, I'll take my coffee back to my desk."

"No, no," Mitch insisted, smoothly guiding her to one of the comfortable chairs. "Jim's right. There's no reason you shouldn't stay and see what you've wrought." His hand was clamped firmly on her elbow, and he gave her a little nudge into the chair, before taking the one beside it.

Jim pushed his glasses up on his nose, smiled vaguely at the two of them, and drew a chair up to where they were sitting. It was a straight-backed chair and he straddled it backwards. Kathryn kept her eyes on Jim's face even after Mitch started talking.

"I don't think you've met the Beresfords—John and Danielle," he told Jim. "They're from Boston, but I met them in California. Actually, they're the ones who convinced me to leave the West Coast and come here to work for them, which I did for several years. Then I broke away and set up Technology Plus on my own. But we've remained friends. No hard feelings from the split."

This seemed perfectly natural to Jim, and he nodded encouragingly. Kathryn stole a quick glance at Mitch, but his expression was so uncompromisingly bland that she switched her gaze to her coffee cup instead.

"It's imperative that we get the security program tested as quickly as possible so we can get it on the market. I'm going to have to bring in a few more people for that."

A puzzled frown formed on Jim's brow. "But we could have it done in a couple of months just with the people we already have."

"That's not good enough. This is the hottest thing we've handled so far, and we can't take a chance of anyone getting an edge on us."

70

Jim shrugged. "Well, it's okay with me. I'll have more time to work on the technical stuff if I don't have to play with the testing—iron out any bugs, that sort of thing."

"Right." Mitch's voice sounded suspiciously hearty. "You're the key person on this project, and the Beresfords want to meet you."

"Meet me?" Jim looked horrified. "What good would that do?"

"If they're putting up venture capital, they want to know whom they're dealing with."

"Surely they'll be dealing with you."

"Yes, but the design of the security system is mainly yours, and they like to know the genius behind the scenes."

This flattery served only to dismay Jim further. "Look, Mitch, I'm not a social type. You can't parade me in front of your rich friends and expect me to bring it off. I wouldn't even know how to talk to them. And they certainly aren't going to understand the intricacies of the security system."

"John will," Mitch assured him. "Danielle isn't as familiar with computers as she is with high finance, but she has a knack for recognizing talent when she runs across it. There's nothing to be alarmed about. It's just cocktails at their house tomorrow evening. You don't have anything else on, do you?"

"I can find something to do," Jim grumbled. "You know I can't talk to people like that."

"There's nothing frightening about them. You just talk to them like you'd talk to anyone else." Mitch offered him a confident smile. "It's no big deal."

"I can't see the point in it," Jim said obstinately, rubbing a finger across the bridge of his nose. "Besides, I don't like cocktails."

Mitch was getting irritable. "You can drink anything you want, for God's sake. It's important that you show up if I'm going to get them to invest in the company."

Jim's gaze happened to fall on the silent Kathryn, and his eyes lit. "Could I take Kathryn with me?"

There was a moment of awkward stillness before Mitch answered in a marvelously level voice. "If you wish. Or anyone else you'd care to bring."

The object of both their eyes, Kathryn squirmed uncomfortably on her chair. Jim was the first to speak.

"What do you say, Kathryn? I'll go if you will."

Mitch looked seriously annoyed. Kathryn didn't know whether he wanted her to refuse or to accept. One of his hands gripped his knee in what must have been a painful hold, and his dark brows gathered together over the green eyes like storm clouds. Well, it was important to him to get Jim there, so she supposed he wanted her to agree. Surely it was the least she could do.

"If it would really be all right with the Beresfords, yes, I'll go. But I don't want to impose."

The storm descended from Mitch's brows to his eyes. "It will be all right with the Beresfords," he said grimly. "Seven-thirty. I'll have Susan leave the address on your desk."

He rose so abruptly he made Jim scoot crablike backwards on the wheels of his chair to get out of the way. Mitch didn't even glance at Kathryn as he said, "I appreciate your coming, Jim. You'll like the Beresfords." Then he nodded briefly at both of them and walked rapidly from the lounge.

Jim grinned at Kathryn. "Maybe he wanted to take you himself."

"Oh, no," she protested. "What he's afraid of is that now there will be two of us who don't know how to conduct ourselves in polite society."

"Two of us?" Jim was genuinely confused. "How could he worry that you'd have the least difficulty?"

"I was raised on a farm."

"So?"

Kathryn laughed. "Well, he seems to think that makes me rather unsophisticated, and I'm afraid he's right."

Jim snorted. "You can talk to people. That's the only thing that's important. I get in a social situation, and the only thing I seem to talk about is computers, which bores just about everyone to tears. And just about everything they talk about bores me to tears."

He looked so gloomy Kathryn felt a surge of sympathy for him. "I'll let you talk to me about computers as much as you want."

"Thanks. But it's not just that. I never know what to wear, either. Actually, I doubt if I even own the right thing to wear. You'll be embarrassed to go with me."

"No, I won't," she insisted. "I'll find out from Susan exactly what's right for the occasion, and we'll both knock their eyes out, even if it means taking you shopping at Brooks Brothers. Would you mind that?"

"Not if you wouldn't mind doing it. I could use something in my closet besides jeans. Every once in a while I have to go to someone's wedding." He looked thoughtful. "Though that doesn't always mean getting dressed up these days, especially if it's in Cambridge."

"I suppose not." Kathryn squeezed his hand and rose. "I'll talk to Susan. Save lunch hour for some shopping."

It was a very strange shopping trip. Jim was totally uninterested in clothes and deferred entirely to Kathryn's judgment, commenting only on whether the blazer or the slacks fit him comfortably and whether he could live with the tie and shirt. The salesman who took them in charge kept referring to Kathryn as Jim's wife. Neither of them bothered to correct him.

To be on the safe side, Kathryn had him buy socks and handkerchiefs, but she couldn't quite bring herself to inquire whether he needed new underwear. They were late coming back to the office because Kathryn remembered he'd probably need shoes as well.

"What about you?" Susan inquired with amusement as Jim walked past loaded down with packages and mumbling to himself.

"I already have something I think will be perfect. It's not new but it's . . ." She hesitated, and her eyes took on a decided twinkle. "It's very sophisticated. Just the sort of thing you suggested."

"Oh, boy. I'll bet. Going to knock old Mitch on his ear, are you?"

Kathryn fluttered her eyelashes. "Why, Susan, I'm going with Jim."

"Jim wouldn't notice if you wore a sack."

"Probably not, but Mitch wouldn't notice unless I wore my hair in braids," Kathryn retorted. "He's bound to think I'll show up in a milkmaid's dress."

Susan regarded her thoughtfully. "Oh, I don't know. Something about you is making him decidedly jumpy."

Kathryn's breath caught in her throat. "Is he . . . well, a woman chaser?"

"No, I wouldn't say so. About average for an eligible bachelor in Boston." Her lips twisted ruefully. "Sometimes I think my husband envies him."

"Nonsense. Married men just like to make their wives feel guilty for 'tying them down,' when usually the shoe's on the other foot. I've seen it with my sister's husband." Kathryn heard an office door open toward the back and sped for the elevator. She had no desire to run into Mitch when she was late.

The doors closed just as he came into sight, and she leaned against the side of the elevator with a sigh of relief—and with the disturbing flutter in her chest that was becoming an annoyingly regular accompaniment to any sight of her boss.

Kathryn took work home that evening to make up for the lost time at lunch. She didn't want to remain alone at the office, in case Mitch should wander around the building after everyone else had left and find her there alone. That would be asking for a repeat of their previous performance in his office, and she wasn't sure she was ready for that—yet.

Somewhere inside her she acknowledged that she

wanted it to happen again, that she ached for his kiss and his touch, but this wild attraction between them had to have a much more solid foundation before she'd be willing to let go again.

She was, after all, a country woman from Vermont. And he was an eligible Boston bachelor. Chances were they didn't look at the episode in the same light. Kathryn had no intention of letting him make an ass of her just because she happened to find herself overwhelmed by the sight of him. Fortitude was one of the virtues any self-respecting farmer's daughter possessed. It seemed a great pity one was called on to use it just when one least wanted to!

When she had finished her work, she wandered into the bedroom and pulled the blue silk dress out of her closet. Fashions changed yearly, even monthly, and she'd bought the dress three years ago. But she knew it was perfect. Nothing else she'd ever owned so flattered her figure or so perfectly matched the deep blue of her eyes.

She removed her dress and slipped the silk one on, loving the soft swish of the fabric as it settled smoothly over her hips. The only mirror in the apartment was in the bathroom over the sink. She had to stand on the rim of the tub to see herself, but she wanted to make sure she wasn't mistaken.

No, it fit just as she remembered, cut low enough over the bosom to be provocative without being too daring. The smooth, rich material clung to every curve, flowing down her body to dance at her knees when she moved.

As it was a little dangerous to move on the tub rim, she hopped to the floor. A price tag swung out from the sleeveless shoulder, and she regarded it with wry humor. Never worn. She'd intended to wear it to Barry's graduation prom and had saved a whole month's salary from her campus job to buy it. Ah, the best laid plans. . . .

In the end she hadn't gone with him. Barry had explained a week before the dance that he absolutely had to take the daughter of a law school professor he'd be having for classes the next year. He'd known she would understand. Well, she had understood just fine, Kathryn thought, making a face at herself in the mirror. And what she'd understood best was that Barry, interested only in what was best to promote his career, was not a man with whom she planned to spend any more time.

She refused to make further comparisons between Barry and Mitch. The silk dress caressed her skin, making her feel almost unbearably feminine. Those country girl hormones acting up again! she thought with a grin. And, whether she liked it or not, Mitch was certainly the man most able to make them go berserk. She sighed and drew the dress over her head. It would be interesting to see what kind of impression it made on the Great Software Entrepreneur. Kathryn was certain it would have no effect whatsoever on Jim.

But Jim surprised her the following day by inviting her out to dinner after work. His choice of restaurant wasn't particularly exciting, and it turned out his main interest was in having her come home with him and make sure he dressed properly. When they arrived at his apartment, Kathryn found the clothes they'd bought still in their bags and boxes, piled on a table already covered with print-outs. She shook her head with amusement and began unwrapping them as he wandered into the bathroom to shower and shave. He didn't bother to close the door.

"Do you have an iron?" she called over the rush of water.

"Hell, I don't know," he replied. "Probably. My mother came by with a whole pile of stuff right after I moved in. Stuff she said I'd need. But I've never used any of it. I just shoved the whole lot in the hall closet to get it out of the way."

Kathryn found an iron and an ironing board in the closet. The shirt and slacks only needed a touch-up, and she was almost finished when Jim emerged from the bathroom in boxer shorts and an undershirt, toweling his hair. "You're not going to make me put any goo on it, are you?" he demanded.

"Of course not," she assured him. "You don't own any, do you?"

"I don't think so. Maybe I should have gotten a haircut."

He seemed perfectly oblivious to his state of undress, so Kathryn, too, ignored it. "Your hair will be fine. Just brush it back the way you usually do."

"Well, actually I don't brush it," he confessed. "I use my fingers."

"Today you brush it."

He shrugged and headed back into the bathroom, to return a minute later looking too tidy, like a small boy ready for a birthday party. Kathryn decided it would probably dry to look much as usual, so she ignored it and handed him the button-down shirt. With a skeptical frown, he accepted it.

"Not my usual sort of thing," he muttered as he thrust his arms through the sleeves.

Kathryn didn't bother to remind him that he'd been with her when they bought it. Instead she handed him the tie. "You're going to look terrific, Jim." But it took a little work. He had a tendency to treat all clothes the same, carelessly. Kathryn smoothed the shirt down over his shoulders, centered the tie, found a belt in his closet for him to wear with the gray slacks and adjusted the blazer at his cuffs. Then she led him to a full-length mirror on the inside of a closet door, which he didn't seem to know he had, and exhibited him. "What did I tell you?"

"God," he muttered, "I look just like Mitch."

Though she didn't agree with this assessment, she smiled. "I hope the shoes aren't going to pinch. New ones are always a nuisance."

They'd chosen loafers because Jim insisted all the others he tried made him feel like a used car salesman. Since the only things he'd had on his feet in the last year were tennis shoes, Kathryn wasn't surprised. But she had more important things to think about now. "We've got to get me home so I can dress," she pointed out.

Jim drove a battered Volkswagen bug whose seats were in need of recovering. Kathryn tried not to think about sitting on them with her lovely silk dress. It was her intention to leave Jim in the car while she dressed, but he waved aside the suggestion, saying, "You may need my help."

She couldn't imagine how, and yet, when time was running out, she called him into the bathroom to assist with the hairstyle she couldn't seem to manage by herself. The long burnished tresses refused to stay in place on the top of her head while she tried to work quickly with the pins. He grinned at her in the mirror. "Going to really do it up, are you? What do you want me to do?"

The braids kept a constant wave in her hair and when she freed them and fluffed them out it made her hair look lusciously full and exotic. By pulling it loosely toward the crown of her head, she was able to leave a mass of curls there, with a few stray ones hanging down on either side in front of her ears.

"Wow!" he exclaimed, stepping back after she'd gotten it securely fastened. "Why don't you wear it that way to the office?"

"It would just be a nuisance. The pins come out if I'm not careful."

Kathryn applied makeup as he stood watching curiously. After a moment, however, he was distracted by the loose shower and said, "Hey, I could fix this in a couple of minutes if you have any tools."

"No, you don't! Not in those clothes!" She shooed him out of the room and swiftly finished up, joining him in the living room with a light coat over her arm.

"You aren't going to need that," he said. "It's hot out."

"It's to protect my dress from your car seat," she informed him tartly. "Hasn't anyone ever objected to the disgraceful condition of your car seats?"

His expression was totally bewildered. "My car seats? Who'd complain about them?"

"Never mind." Kathryn laughed and took his arm. "Just get me there in one piece, and I'll never mention them again."

He was an absent-minded driver, to say the least. Kathryn decided some minutes later that it would have been easier to leave the car parked outside her apartment and walk. The Beresfords had a lovely red brick house on Chestnut Street, an area of Beacon Hill where there was only resident parking.

Eventually Jim squeezed the battered VW between two carelessly parked cars and, unsure of his social etiquette, trotted Kathryn four blocks to the elegant house so they wouldn't be late.

They were admitted by a butler. Jim threw a panicky look at Kathryn; she merely smiled demurely back at him. It wasn't as if she'd run into a butler in the course of her twenty-four years, either, but she certainly wasn't going to act as though that were the case. She'd left her coat in the car, so there was no need to do more than follow the fellow up a handsome flight of stairs to an immense room, lushly carpeted and filled with fragile-looking antiques. There were already three people in the room; Mitch was one of them. Kathryn forced her attention to the other two as she and Jim were announced.

John Beresford was a man of about fifty, of only medium height, with steel gray hair and shrewd eyes. His wife, Danielle, was dressed in an off-the-shoulder dress of flaming oranges and reds that Kathryn had no difficulty believing could have been purchased in Paris. Though Mrs. Beresford was probably her husband's age, she gave the impression of being considerably younger. As she came forward with outstretched hands, she somehow conveyed an air of French sophistication, rather than the proper Bostonian image her husband radiated.

"Miss Lambert! So pleased to meet you." Her eyes

glowed with approval as she took in Kathryn's blue silk dress. "Mitch has told us a bit about you, dear. And this is Jim Zachary with you. Mitch says you're one of the shining lights at Technology Plus, Mr. Zachary."

Jim flushed under her admiring gaze. "How do you do, Mrs. Beresford?" He managed to mumble a greeting to Mr. Beresford as well, shaking his hand with a firmness his host may not have appreciated.

Mitchell had strolled across the room after them, and though he greeted Jim warmly, his eyes seemed glued to Kathryn. The expression on his face was almost comical. He couldn't have looked more stunned if Cinderella had been transformed before his eyes.

"Mitchell." Kathryn's tone was pleasant as she extended a hand for his clasp. She found the hand gripped firmly between both of his, but the sensation was not one of friendly warmth. He was tugging her out of earshot of the other three people. "Dear me," she murmured in her best social voice. "Have I done something wrong?"

"Where did you learn how to dress like that?" he demanded.

"Why, in Vermont, of course. Is there something wrong with it?"

His snapping green eyes traveled from the winsome curls on the crown of her head to the perfectly acceptable shoes on her small feet. "You know there isn't," he said gruffly. "You look fantastic."

"Thank you." From the corner of her eye she could see that Jim was in need of moral support. His shoulders were hunched forward defensively as his host and hostess questioned him. "Excuse me, Mitchell. I really should go to Jim's rescue."

Mitchell tore his eyes away from her for a brief moment. "He'll be all right. They aren't going to gobble him up."

"I promised," she told him stubbornly, turning toward the threesome, who were drifting across to a wet bar where the butler awaited their drink orders.

Kathryn couldn't quite catch what it was Mitchell growled, but she ignored it. She'd seen Jim look back over his shoulder, a pleading expression on his face, and she hurried to catch up with the others. Mr. Beresford asked her what she was having to drink, and she chose a glass of sherry.

There were two matching Sheraton sofas and several Hepplewhite chairs grouped around a fireplace opposite the wet bar. Danielle Beresford tucked her hand in the crook of Jim's arm and led him there. Her husband turned his attention to Kathryn, which left Mitch trailing behind them, looking chagrined, especially when each of the couples claimed one of the sofas and he was left to take one of the none-too-comfortable chairs.

"There will be a few other people coming later," Danielle was explaining to Jim, "but we wanted to have a chance to meet you first."

If this was supposed to flatter or please him, Jim gave no sign that it served its purpose. He was in the process of loosening his tie, his glass of beer gripped firmly in his other hand. Thinking something was expected of him, he finally murmured, "It was nice of you to have me, ma'am."

"Please call me Danielle," she said with a friendly smile.

Kathryn was fascinated by the way Danielle continued to introduce and drop topics in an effort to find something that caught Jim's fancy. There were remarks on the opera, a recent concert, two plays, and a series of movies, before she moved on to sports. Jim showed not the slightest interest in baseball, football, basketball, tennis, or golf. To Kathryn's immense surprise, his eyes lit up when his hostess mentioned her sailboat.

"Where do you sail?" he asked. "How big a boat is it? Where do you keep it?"

Danielle laughed, pleased with her hard-won success, and relayed every bit of information she could think of.

"Would you like to come out with us? We're planning to sail on Saturday. Miss Lambert, too, of course."

The offer was eagerly accepted by Jim, who included Kathryn in his acceptance almost absently. When John Beresford queried her with raised eyebrows, she nodded.

Mitchell coughed.

"But of course you're invited, Mitch," Danielle teased. "You're one of the family."

The butler appeared in the doorway of the room to announce the arrival of another couple, and the Beresfords excused themselves, leaving Kathryn, Jim, and Mitch each seated separately in the conversation area. Mitch was the first to move, lithely springing up from his chair to capture the space beside Kathryn on the sofa. Jim didn't even seem to notice.

"That was nice of them," Jim said earnestly to Kathryn. "You want to go, don't you?"

"It sounds like fun." She was very aware that Mitch's arm rested along the back of the sofa, although he made no attempt to touch her shoulders. "I've never been sailing."

"You'll love it!" Jim's eyes were bright with anticipation, but a small frown appeared above them. "I suppose they wear something fancy, though. You might have to help me dress again."

Mitchell's voice rapped into the silence that followed this remark. "Jeans and tennis shoes will be adequate for sailing with the Beresfords, Jim. There's no need for Kathryn to be involved."

Kathryn blinked at his fierce tone. "I don't mind helping Jim. In fact, he was a big help to *me*."

"She has the most amazing hair," Jim informed Mitch with absolutely no malice intended. "It's so thick your hands get lost in it. No wonder she can't find the right place for pins."

Mitchell surveyed Kathryn's hair with decided partiality and a smoldering light in his eyes. "Kathryn should learn to fix her own hair. You're not always going to be around to do it for her." This last sounded more like a command than a statement.

"Well," Jim mused, tugging at the cuffs of his blazer, but totally unaware of his employer's annoyance, "she doesn't wear it that way very often. With a little practice, she could probably do it herself. I think it was because we were rushed there at the end."

Things seemed to be going from bad to worse. Kathryn would have been glad enough to straighten out the misunderstanding if Mitchell hadn't been acting so positively dictatorial. She was relieved when Danielle appeared before them with two more guests and both men were forced to stand. Within minutes the cocktail party was swirling around them, and she found herself separated from both Jim and Mitchell for the next hour.

Only one thing of significance to her happened during that time, and it was overhearing John Beresford tell Mitch that he and his wife would indeed be interested in purchasing part ownership of Technology Plus. "Your Jim is a bright fellow, and I think his security system has every chance of capturing the market. Don't lose him," he remarked with a paternal pat on Mitch's shoulder.

It made Kathryn nervous to think that so much was riding on Jim, especially when she had left the way open to his being headhunted by Roger Owens. Well, perhaps that wasn't the only thing that made her nervous. As she wandered around the room, frequently coming to Jim's aid when he got stuck with people who didn't talk computers, she tended to follow Mitchell around with her eyes. He was usually talking with a woman.

Much as she told herself this shouldn't bother her, she couldn't help feeling a twinge of envy. He did not come to her at all until just after Jim had suggested he was ready to leave. Then Mitchell appeared at her side, putting a possessive arm around her shoulders.

"I'll take Kathryn home," he announced. "There's no need for you to bother."

Jim looked bewildered. "It's no bother."

"It's out of your way," Mitch said smoothly.

Both Kathryn and Jim knew he lived in the penthouse at Technology Plus. Kathryn's apartment was in quite the opposite direction, if not far. Still, she was irritated with him for the proprietary air he was using, and the way he'd avoided her all evening, so she slipped out from under his arm. "Thank you, Mitchell, but I'll go home with Jim." That sounded like the start of another misunderstanding, so she added quickly, "I mean, he'll take me home. My coat's in his car."

"Right," Jim agreed, nodding. "So it is. Well, good night, Mitch. See you in the morning."

It sounded so much like Kathryn's own dismissal of him the night he'd come to her apartment that she had to catch her lip between her teeth to keep from laughing.

He was not amused. She could tell by the flare in his eyes, but he made no attempt to stop them. At the doorway Kathryn looked back to see him frowning. She offered a tentative smile, which was not returned.

6

Jim's car was not conducive to relaxing. After the strains of the evening, Kathryn would have liked to sink back against the seat and let her nerves recover, but when she put her elbow on the armrest, it broke loose. Kathryn raised her voice to be heard over the hiccuping rattle of the engine. "How long have you had this gem?"

"The car? Since I was a senior in college. Neat, huh?"

"I don't think *neat* is the word, Jim. Something like *funky* might be better."

Jim grinned at her and revved the motor, causing it to make a popping sound in addition to the rest of its symphony of odd noises. "The muffler needs replacing, but the car is fundamentally sound." He jutted his head forward to listen. "I'm a little worried about the transmission, but I fixed the carburetor myself last week."

"It sounds like you should consider getting a new car," she remarked, remembering too late what he'd told her about his financial problems.

"Not until it falls apart. When I have extra money, I like to spend it on sailing. Can you imagine having a boat the size of the Beresfords'?"

Kathryn couldn't, but she felt a surge of sympathy for him as he hunched over the wheel, peering out the windshield. "Your security program is going to make a lot of money for Tech Plus. Why don't you ask for a raise?"

Jim pulled up in the only available space, by a fire hydrant, and with a final hiccup, the little car came to rest. In the light from a nearby streetlamp, Kathryn could see a small frown crease his brow. "It hardly seems fair, when Mitch just had to borrow money to speed up production of the program. Still, there will be more money now . . . and I had to buy all these clothes to impress his investors." He glanced down at the blazer, which was already, like most of his clothes, looking a little rumpled.

A coldness gripped Kathryn's heart. Was Mitch taking advantage of Jim's position? It would explain why he was so concerned that someone could easily steal Jim away from the company. She so wanted to believe in the integrity of the man who could stir her senses more strongly than any man ever had. But she'd always known there was reason to distrust him, hadn't she?

The one thing she'd learned during that session in Mitchell's office was that she was just as vulnerable to losing her head as any woman. Her treacherous memory allowed a fleeting replay of those moments in his strong male arms. Then she shook her head fiercely to clear it.

Roused from the abstraction he'd fallen into, Jim peered apologetically at her through his glasses, looking more storklike than ever. "Sorry, Kathryn, I was thinking. Guess I've exhausted my store of social graces for the evening."

He unfolded himself from behind the wheel, got out, and came around to her side of the car. Her door gave a metallic squeal of protest and sagged alarmingly when he opened it. He shook his head ruefully.

Gathering her coat as she climbed out, Kathryn didn't

meet his eyes when she said, "You might talk to Mitch about a raise."

Jim responded with a negligent shrug as he walked her to the door, but just as she was about to slip in, he murmured, "I might."

Alone in her apartment, Kathryn spent a long time thinking about Mitchell and the difference between his life-style and Jim's. Of course, there were differences between the two men, but that hardly accounted for everything. It seemed quite possible to her that Mitchell wasn't paying Jim what he was worth, but there was no way for her to know. With a heavy heart, she removed the lovely blue silk dress and hung it far back in the closet.

Jim was quiet and more abstracted than usual the following day. He spent some time doodling on a pad instead of at the computer and, passing behind him to look for a memory disk, Kathryn saw the outlines of a graceful sailing vessel on the scratch pad. When he saw her looking he grinned self-consciously and crumpled up the page.

Mitchell only came upstairs twice during the day. Each time, he sent a smoldering glance her way, his mouth firmly fixed and his eyes aloof. When he stopped at Jim's office just at quitting time and cast an especially intent look her way, Kathryn decided discretion was the better part of valor. She retrieved her purse from her desk as unobtrusively as possible, afraid he might offer to take her home. His mocking glance as he observed her action told her he had no such intention. As she left, the two men were engaged in a low-voiced discussion.

So much for any illusions that Mitchell was really interested in her, she thought gloomily. Since she'd shown herself unwilling to carry things quite as far as he might like, well, he was ready to forget the whole thing. Far from relieving her mind, the thought made a lump rise in her throat, and she unaccountably felt like crying. That in turn made her angry, so she set herself a task that would take her mind off the aggravating source of her tension.

On her way home from work she purchased a gallon can of paint and a bag of painting supplies. That would certainly keep her busy. When there was work to be done, there was no cause for giving in to any weak-kneed susceptibility to a mere man!

Two hours later, she was feeling weak-kneed, but for an altogether different reason. She had managed to apply the cream-colored paint to the cracked ceiling of the small living room, getting only the usual amount spattered on her head, and was now working on the first wall. The plastic drop cloth she'd purchased was spread over the nubby green sofa and floor.

Painting was harder than she'd thought. She took a breather, perching carefully on the draped arm of the sofa. Holding the dripping roller in one hand, she wiped her perspiring forehead with the other arm, managing only to leave a broad streak of paint there. The cream color was a vast improvement on the dingy beige, she decided as she surveyed the room. By the time she'd completed the job it should look quite nice. Her musings were interrupted by a buzz from her doorbell. Stepping cautiously on the slippery plastic drop cloth, she walked to the door and opened it with the chain on.

"Mitchell!" she exclaimed. Her pulse began to hammer and a flush worked its way up her throat to her cheeks. So much for work therapy, she thought morosely.

"Open the door, Kathryn. I want to talk to you." His voice sounded grim.

"This isn't a convenient time, Mitchell," she replied haughtily.

Quick anger flashed on his face. "Open the door, Kathryn! Convenient or not, I have something to say to you, and it won't keep."

"All right," she agreed grudgingly. Slipping the chain, she stood back to let him enter.

He strode in like an angry panther, only to stop short and stare, his eyes moving from the disorder of the room to her own messy condition. His eyes widened, and his wrathful expression dissolved into startled mirth.

Indignant at his shout of laughter, Kathryn glared at him. "Haven't you ever seen anyone doing honest labor before?"

"Have you seen yourself in a mirror? Nobody looking at that face could help but laugh. What do you think you're doing?"

"What does it look like?" she retorted, dropping the roller in its tray and edging toward the bathroom. "The circus has an opening for a clown, and I'm rehearsing for the part." She darted into the bathroom and grabbed a washcloth to do what she could with the paint on her face.

He came and leaned against the doorway. "You'll have to do a full wash job on that hair." He put his head to one side speculatively. "You can tell what you'll look like when you're an old lady."

They both regarded her reflection in the mirror over the sink. Her hair and eyelashes were generously sprinkled. Since she'd put on an old long-sleeved man's shirt, her arms had been protected, but below her denim cutoffs, her legs had somehow acquired several smears.

Mitchell grinned at her. "You know, you're the most colorful woman I know." His gaze traveled from the cream-sprinkled red of her hair to the sparkling blue of her eyes. "I thought when I first saw you in that barn that you could look pretty spectacular, but I must say you've outdone yourself."

Her breast heaved in indignation, but she forgot what she was going to say when Mitchell's eyes followed the movement and kindled into something other than amusement. Backing away the few inches allowed by the tiny bathroom, she returned his suddenly intent stare with a warning toss of her head.

"Don't worry," he mocked. "Until you remove a few

layers of that paint, you're safe with me. I don't suppose you'd like to take a shower now, would you?" At the withering look she gave him, he went on regretfully, "I didn't think so. Pity. But then I don't think that rickety shower would stand up to two people using it at the same time."

It was clear it wouldn't take much to make him forget the paint. Dropping the wet washcloth, Kathryn eased past him out of the confining space. He followed her into the living room, where she backed warily toward the can of paint and the roller.

"Why did you come here, Mitchell?" she asked, tilting her chin pugnaciously at him.

He had to think for a second; then his brow darkened and his face resumed its angry expression. "I think you might be able to guess. What have you been saying to Jim?"

She looked blank. "What?"

"I had a long talk with him. In the middle of a whole lot of guff about carburetors and boats, Jim managed to get across the idea that you seem to think he should have a raise."

"So what? Maybe I do."

"What does it have to do with you? Are you lining him up as a marriage prospect and want to make sure he's worth it?"

Kathryn's temper rose to match his. She tilted her head back so she could look scathingly over, if not down, her nose at him. "I wouldn't aim so high. But it would be nice to ride in a car that stayed in one piece for the whole evening."

He glared at her. "I'm telling you to stay out of matters that don't concern you. My financial arrangements with Jim are none of your business."

Kathryn snorted. "I don't think much of a financial arrangement where you ride around in a Mercedes and Jim makes do with an old heap from his college days!"

As soon as the words were out, she wished she'd swallowed them instead.

Cold dignity masked his face as he started toward the door. Kathryn instinctively put her hand on his arm to stop him. His skin felt warm beneath her touch. "I shouldn't have said that, Mitchell. I'm sorry."

He looked down at her hand, then into her eyes. "I'm not cheating Jim, if that's what you mean. He gets a fair salary."

"But Tech Plus is going to make a lot of money from his program."

"Maybe. Any number of things could go wrong. You're in the big leagues now. Isn't that what you called it? And in the big leagues nothing is as simple as it appears." His eyes narrowed. "Maybe a lot of things aren't as simple as they seem."

Mesmerized by his intent look, Kathryn blinked up at him, her blue eyes wide and serious.

"Sometimes you look so innocent," he said gruffly. "Other times you go out of your way to provoke me. And all the time I'd swear you're laughing at me. I've come to think the only way to get at the truth about you is to do this . . ."

She started to step away from him, but it was too late. He reached for her, one hand tilting her head toward his lips, the other about her waist, drawing her closer.

"You . . . you'll get paint all over you!" she gasped.

"Thanks for the warning," he whispered, his breath warm on her skin as he began to explore her mouth. His hand moved from her waist to the front of her shirt, deftly unfastening buttons.

"Now, look here, Mitchell!"

"Why, thank you," he replied, easing back the cloth of the paint-covered shirt. "Relax. I won't hurt you. This is just a kind of experiment." When she didn't immediately object, he slid his arms around her.

Almost hypnotized by his gentle touch and amazed at

his audacity, Kathryn delayed a little too long before she opened her mouth to protest. As though her parted lips were the invitation he had been waiting for, he promptly closed them with his own.

His mouth molded and teased her own soft lips, tempting her to relax and enjoy the sensations being aroused. Kathryn forgot her intention to call an immediate halt to this bold seduction. Why shouldn't she experiment just a little? She was curious, too. She slipped her arms free and threaded her fingers through the hair at the back of his head. To increase her enjoyment, she then exerted her own influence on the way their mouths were moving together.

His hands moved in caressing strokes over the smooth surface of her back, sending tingling sensations shooting through her. When his supple fingers began to sweep the curves of her breasts, his thumbs brushing the swelling curves just above the lace of her bra, a dizziness overcame her that made her wonder vaguely if she were going to faint. Her fingers dug into his unruly hair, pulling him closer.

He responded by liberating her breasts and pulling her into a more urgent embrace, his kiss seeking to join every surface of their warm, moist mouths. The feeling of his lightly clad body against hers was incredibly arousing. She was conscious of his belt buckle pressing against the bare skin of her stomach, and daring, erotic thoughts rioted through her brain.

She had to stop this. "Don't," she breathed, breaking off the mind-destroying kiss.

"Do, you mean," he said, his voice as breathless as hers. "Hold on tight. Here we go again . . ."

And she did hold on, her hands clutching at him through the fine weave of his shirt as his persuasive mouth captured hers once more. Nothing existed except the honey sweetness of his mouth and his tongue teaching her things she was eager to learn. He whispered to her, his lips skimming over her face and throat.

His hands duplicated this touch, skimming over her body, sensitizing every bare inch. What he was saying didn't register. She tried to concentrate, but when he pulled her hard against his thighs and his voice turned thick, she knew the experiment had gone more than far enough. Kathryn strained away from him, which only made his arms tighten to keep her firmly locked against him. His head came down to hers once more, his lips eagerly parted.

"No," she insisted, straining in an effort to avoid the kiss. "This isn't what I want!" She stumbled backward as his grip loosened, and he moved quickly to steady her. Unfortunately, the soles of his shoes were slick, and they slid on the plastic drop cloth. Off-balance, he teetered for a moment. Kathryn watched in astonishment as he crashed to the floor in a welter of flying arms and legs, paint can, and roller tray. Creamy white paint slopped over the rim of the can to soak into his linen slacks.

When the reverberations of the fall had died away, there was silence. Kathryn stared, wide-eyed, at the spectacle on the floor. Her lips twitched. Crinkles appeared at the corners of her eyes. Finally her pretty mouth opened, showing even, white teeth, and she threw her head back, allowing gales of laughter to erupt.

His face flushed, Mitchell stared at her grimly as the peals rang out over him. When her mirth was reduced to hiccupping gasps, he rose with offended dignity and shook out his slacks. The paint did not shake off.

"I think," Kathryn gasped, "there might be a job for a male clown, too, if you're . . . interested!"

For a moment she thought a battle was raging inside him. His chest began to shake; his head turned from side to side. Then an "Oof!" escaped him, followed by another. The sounds multiplied into a series of chuckles that ended in an explosion of laughter. Her rippling treble joined his bass. When they were reduced to fits and starts, Mitchell wiped his streaming eyes, leaving a streak of paint that threatened to set them off again.

"What is this built-in protection you have against my best seduction attempts?" he asked finally in resignation. "That's not the way it's supposed to go, you know."

"Really?" she returned innocently. "I thought it went very well."

"So did I, at first."

"It went far enough. I don't want to play that kind of game, Mitch."

He reached for a cleaning rag and attempted to remove some of the wet paint from his hands. "And here I thought you were good at games." His green eyes glinted as he noted the way she was clutching her shirt together over her breasts. "We could share a shower," he suggested hopefully.

Kathryn looked pointedly at the door. "If I were you, I'd get home to my own shower as fast as I could . . . and step in with my clothes on. That paint's going to dry quickly."

He grinned at her. "Have it your way this time, my red-headed farmer's daughter. But I'll be doing some mustache-twirling come the weekend when we take that trip to Marblehead. Better be on guard." Stepping cautiously over the mess on the floor, he reached down and picked up the paint roller. "Looks like your paint's all gone. If you give me a call, I'll be glad to come over another day and help you."

She took the roller from him. "No, thanks. I can finish the job myself."

"Then I'll have to pin my hopes on Marblehead."

"As long as you don't pin them on me," she retorted, her blue eyes sparkling. "Are we all driving over together, Jim and you and I?"

He took his time answering, shooting her a glance from under frowning brows. "You want Jim along? Why?"

"He might not get there otherwise. I'm surprised we made it back to my apartment last night."

Mitchell stiffened. "You mean he didn't get any farther? Just how late did he stay?"

"That has nothing to do with you."

"I'm responsible to your uncle for seeing you don't get mixed up with more than you can handle."

"Ha! Coming from you, that's like the fox worrying about the chicken catching cold in the draft from the open hen house door."

An offended look settled over the handsome face. "I most certainly care about your welfare." He stalked to the door and used the cleaning rag to open it. "Can I take this with me? I don't want to mess up my car."

Kathryn picked up an old newspaper from the stack she'd collected for her painting. "You'd better take this, too. For sitting on," she explained, her eyes alive with merriment.

He took it from her with an aloof expression. "Well, how long *did* he stay?"

"Just long enough to drop me off. He didn't dare leave the car on the street too long. Someone might have stolen it. An antique like that is pretty valuable, you know."

His flashing grin rewarded her. "As the owner of a Mercedes, I know I'm suspect, but my guess is that Jim wouldn't buy a new car even if he had the money. The man's boat crazy. But you're probably right about his getting to Marblehead. I'll pick him up before I come for you."

His lean hands came to capture her shoulders, pulling her to him. His green eyes moved almost tenderly over her face, and he dropped a kiss on her cheek, where a spatter of paint remained. "What is it about you?" he murmured huskily. "I never see you without wanting to do something like this." His mouth brushed hers with a zephyr-light kiss.

Kathryn's lips trembled with the sweetness of the kiss. The faint response reignited his still-smoldering passion.

His mouth hardened and moved hungrily on hers; his arms tightened to imprint her form against his.

A protesting moan sounded from Kathryn's throat, and with an echoing protestation from his own throat, he broke off the incendiary contact and set her away from him. His smile reflected the regret he felt at ending the interlude. When he saw her shake her head slightly but adamantly, he smiled again ruefully, and left without a word. Part of a white footprint near the door was all that remained from his explosive visit.

By the time Saturday arrived, Kathryn was looking forward to the trip to Marblehead. Her normal good spirits enabled her to push aside the emotion-arousing effects of Mitchell's visit. In fact, by the time she'd purchased more paint and finished the job in the living room, she'd managed to convince herself she was in control of the situation.

Mitchell was on to her "farmer's daughter" routine but had taken it in good part, even going along with the game in his "mustache-twirling" seduction attempts. At the office over the last few days, he'd delivered several outrageous innuendos that apparently gave him ample enjoyment, considering his wicked grins. Had she ever thought she knew all the "farmer's daughter" jokes there were? Obviously he was capable of coming up with some new ones.

Mitchell and Jim arrived early Saturday morning to pick her up. After a quick but comprehensive glance at Mitchell, immaculate in white nautical shirt and pants and devastating smile, she turned to inspect Jim's turn-out.

"Morning, Kathryn," he greeted her, awkwardly adjusting his glasses. His unexpectedly sweet smile appeared, and Kathryn responded to it, again feeling a surge of liking for him. He was dressed in old denims, faded but clean, with a new shirt, red and blue striped, still showing the packaging creases.

"Let's hit the road," Mitchell said curtly.

Kathryn found him glaring at her and glanced quickly down at her outfit. The trim blue linen slacks and delicately embroidered cotton top seemed to be in order. Deck shoes were perfectly appropriate. Probably it was the braids, hanging over her shoulders and tied with crystal buttons in the shape of daisies. She shrugged and slid into the front seat of the Mercedes, while he held the door and glowered. When her sunhat slipped out onto the sidewalk he picked it up and thrust it onto her lap without a word.

Jim climbed in the back, looking preoccupied. Kathryn assumed his mind was still busy with the calculations that had kept him hard at work all Friday and turned to the taciturn Mitchell as he started the car and drove away from the curb.

"You're in a great mood," she teased. "Is something wrong?"

He glanced at her, then at the early morning traffic. When he looked her way again, he smiled. "Not a thing. It looks like a great day for sailing."

Since the sun was shining, the sky was clear, and there was some lessening of the humidity, she supposed he was right. "Have you done enough sailing to know?" she asked provocatively.

"I've done more surfing than sailing."

"Just what I'd expect from a Californian." Turning on the comfortable leather seat, Kathryn tucked one ankle up under her and propped an elbow on the back of the seat, making it easier to study his face as he talked. "Do you miss the West Coast?"

He shrugged. "One coast is pretty much like the other, if you spend most of your time in offices."

"You didn't get your tan in an office."

"I like to run in the mornings." They turned a corner and Mitchell braked suddenly, barely avoiding a child in a street game. Waving his hand to acknowledge the impudent outthrust tongue of the near-victim, he drove calmly on through the residential section.

"Where do you run? Since you live in the penthouse at Tech Plus, doesn't it seem odd to start off on a busy street like Boylston? I'd think the carbon monoxide would cancel any benefits of running."

"I run early, before the cars really get started . . . not on Boylston. The Common's not that far away. It's pleasant there and makes for a good run."

"Do you like living in the same building where you work?" she asked curiously.

"It has its advantages." He flashed her a mocking look. "You really should come up and see for yourself. I've invited you."

Jim spoke from the back seat. "It's a neat place. You should see how he's got it fixed up."

Kathryn was busy pretending that Mitch's invitation was the same as Jim thought it was. That grin of his, however, made it clear he was well aware she had taken his true meaning.

They finally broke free of the city's congestion and the Mercedes began to eat the miles on the throughway north. Fall colors were more evident now, with trees and shrubs along the way showing bits of crimson and gold. Though the scenery was delightful, Kathryn found the man seated next to her even more interesting.

"I got the impression the Beresfords look on you as some sort of fair-haired lad," she probed. "You must have been a real whiz kid if they went to all the trouble of bringing you out here to work for them."

He ignored her lead and picked up a digression, smiling blandly at her. "Do I have the look of a fair-haired lad?"

"At least you've got the freckles," she teased.

"Two of a kind, aren't we? Where'd you get yours?"

"My grandparents were Scots." She wrinkled her nose, not at all bothered by her freckles. "I guess I came

off lightly. Grandpa was practically one solid freckle."
She stopped him as he opened his mouth to comment.
"If you dare say anything faintly resembling the word
cute, I'll never speak to you again!"

"Listen, my little country charmer. Anyone with freckles who wears braids and has eyes as big and blue as
yours is just asking to be called cute." One hand lifted
from the steering wheel and flicked the auburn rope
hanging over the shoulder nearest him. "But I saw for
myself just how you can change from wholesome to
gorgeous, and without the benefit of a fairy godmother.
Your secret's out, and I don't think I'll be calling you . . .
cute." His grin promised much, and his eyes danced with
a pleasant memory.

Feeling as though she'd drifted out of safe depths,
Kathryn said the first thing that came into her head. "But
I did have a fairy godmother, didn't I, Jim?" Half turning
in her seat, she threw their silent companion a reminis-
cent smile. "Jim saved the day, managing to control this
mass of obstinate hair."

"It wasn't so bad." Jim stirred and eased his long legs
into another position. "There isn't much room in that
bathroom, though, for what we were doing. Hey, Mitch,
watch where you're going!"

The Mercedes had swerved but was quickly brought
under control. Kathryn saw Mitchell's hands tighten on
the wheel and heard him swear softly under his breath.
He cast a fulminating look her way, his face gone hard
and truculent.

"It sounds like fun," he said between clenched teeth.
"But there's plenty of room there, if you have a little
imagination."

This remark, made in anger, was not like the teasing
innuendos he'd been delivering at the office. Kathryn felt
a blush rise up her throat and bloom on her cheeks.
"Some people have too much imagination."

"Some don't have enough. Out of many a man's

dreams of today come the realities of tomorrow." He dropped a hand to her thigh, sensuously stroking her through the linen slacks.

Her hand flew downwards to push his aside. Baring her teeth in what passed for a sweet smile, her eyes flashing, she said, "But mostly their dreams are illusions."

Jim had been following their quick, electrically charged exchange. There was a puzzled frown on his forehead as he noted Kathryn's unease. During the rest of the short drive to Marblehead, his thoughtful glance rested on Mitchell more than once. When the Mercedes stopped at the top of the hill overlooking the harbor, he jumped out to help Kathryn alight for a view of the stunning scene below them.

7

⟡⟡⟡⟡⟡⟡⟡⟡⟡

The harbor at Marblehead was like nothing she'd ever seen. Kathryn stared in wonder at what must have been hundreds of boats, dinghys, and yachts spread across the half-mile-wide, mile-long gap that was one of Massachusetts' finest harbors.

"When you come on it unexpectedly, it can give you quite a thrill." Mitchell had come to join her. "The one time I was here before, I came over that hill and almost ran off the road."

"It's glorious!" she exclaimed, her gaze returning to the feast of dazzling color. Bits of white hulls and sails contrasted sharply with pieces of blue water. The sun's rays were reflected at a multitude of points by the brightwork. Flags and tags of all hues fluttered from every conceivable hanging place. She glanced up at the tall man beside her and smiled.

His hand clasped her shoulder. The tension and temper of moments ago had vanished. A feeling of accord flowed between them, and Kathryn felt exquisitely happy.

Jim cleared his throat. "We'll want to take advantage of this early breeze, if we're going sailing."

"Right!" Mitchell looked suddenly carefree. He swept Kathryn companionably into the crook of his arm, guiding her back to the car. "Let's go swing from a yardarm or something."

As she was bundled into the front seat, Kathryn giggled. "If that's all you know about what to do on a sailboat, we're in trouble."

"What I don't know about sailing can be stuffed in a walnut," he bragged, his eyes dancing. "Right, Jim?"

"First I've heard of it. You've never even come out on my little sloop."

Their bantering lasted all the way to the dock space, where a young man met them with a power launch.

"Mr. and Mrs. Beresford have already taken the *BelleFemme* out to the neck of the harbor." Even over the sound of the motor his nasal twang was evident. "They wanted to save time in getting underway."

The launch slid neatly between yachts of every size, shape, and color. Names painted on sterns and sides revealed places of origin, and sometimes lamentable wit. But above all there was the impression of wealth and privilege.

Kathryn glanced at Jim. His expression was not one of envy, but of intent concentration as he studied the variety of craft around him. He caught her gaze and smiled, his eyes bright.

"I can hardly wait! Imagine sailing one of these babies around the Cape."

Mitchell spoke abruptly, pointing. "There it is. To your right, Jim."

"Off the starboard bow you mean, Mitch." Jim grinned cheerfully at his boss. "Wow! What a beauty!"

About thirty-five feet long, the yacht looked sleek and swift, its low, rakish lines favorable for either cruising or racing. John and Danielle Beresford were waiting for them, smiling a welcome. Kathryn made the transfer aboard without mishap, but Mitchell was not so fortunate. A strong swell lifted the yacht as he boarded, and for a moment he fought to keep his balance. Jim grabbed his arm just in time to save him from toppling over the low railing.

"This is no place for a swim," John Beresford teased as he clasped Mitchell's hand, then drew him down into the roomy cockpit in the stern. The two men were dressed similarly, in trim trousers of denim-type fabric and pullover cotton shirts, but John's shirt had small blue anchors on the collar, and he wore a sailor's cap.

"Don't I know it," Mitchell replied, accepting the kiss Danielle bestowed on his cheek. "I went swimming off a beach not far from here once and almost froze my . . . bones."

Danielle greeted Jim and Kathryn with a kiss as well. "Welcome aboard, my dears," she said, as gracious and charming on the yacht as at her home. Her hair, neatly tied up in a brilliant pink silk scarf, set off her coloring and the simple white denims and crewing shirt she wore. She looked exquisite and perfectly comfortable.

"You're smart to protect that lovely skin, Kathryn," she said, looking approvingly at the long sleeves of Kathryn's blouse and the sun hat with its scarf to keep it firmly in place. "Sit with me while the men get the sails up. Ever since I got knocked overboard, I've insisted on the job of helmsman. Now I sit safely in the stern. Later I'll show you around belowdecks."

Kathryn found a place on the upholstered seating that encircled the cockpit, a large, well-like opening, and settled back to watch. The length of the yacht was dominated by the enormously tall mainmast and its sail-furled boom. Complicated rigging made walking on the smooth-surfaced deck a matter of dodging and ducking to escape entanglement.

Jim leaped eagerly into the middle of it all and, at

John's invitation, took over the hoisting of the jib sail. Mitchell was directed to take up a position at the main halyard winch.

"Such a handsome man, don't you think, Kathryn?" Danielle asked, her voice casual, her eyes twinkling.

Kathryn had been watching Mitchell and knew it was to him her hostess referred. She smiled guardedly at Danielle, who continued, lowering her voice confidentially.

"Too involved in his career, though. Our *enfant terrible* needs the right woman to bring him about, I think. There's more to life than business."

Danielle smiled again, apparently not expecting an answer from the embarrassed Kathryn, and turned her attention to the tiller.

The Beresfords took their sailing seriously. The yacht was fitted with every device to enhance the sailing experience without depriving its owners of the joys of personally handling the vessel. Danielle was expert at controlling the tiller, and John, with Jim's help, made easy work of setting the mainsail.

Mitchell found himself slightly in the way. Whatever jobs there were to handle seemed ably handled by the other two. After he had managed to get one of the lines tangled in an effort to help, he dropped down into the cockpit next to Kathryn.

Eyes sparkling, Kathryn grinned at him, her freckles a faint sprinkle of gold dust in the shade from her sun hat. "Isn't this fabulous, Mitch?" She leaned forward to feel the breeze, which increased as they gained speed. The sails, high and curving, billowed out with the invisible forces that filled them, and the sloop heeled several degrees. "Just look at Jim!" she cried.

Jim was moving with angular grace to secure the fastenings of the huge sail. Danielle maneuvered the tiller and *BelleFemme* went winging across the choppy waters like a low-flying gull, the hull at an angle that made them all shift their weight to keep balance. The wind whipped at them with fresh crispness.

Behind his glasses, Jim's eyes were alight with pleasure. His body was arched, his arms extended and strong as they manipulated the lines controlling the angle of the mainsail. "How do you like it, Kathryn?" he called, an immense grin stretching his mouth.

"It's wonderful! Like nothing else in the world."

John carefully balanced his way to the cockpit and lowered himself to the companionway into the cabin extending belowdecks. Before disappearing from view, he paused to inform them, "We're heading for a little place called Tranter's Island. We'll stop there for lunch. Danielle, why don't you give Mitchell a turn at the tiller?"

Danielle gestured for Mitchell to move beside her. "You heard John, Mitch darling. Everyone should learn how to steer a boat. First you, then Kathryn. Put your hands on the tiller, here."

"Maybe I should just watch for a while," he said dubiously. They were well outside the harbor, and the seas were brisk, with spray flying from the bow.

"Nonsense. It's very simple. Just push the tiller in the opposite direction to where you want to go."

Mitchell gripped the long wooden handle tightly. "The opposite direction, did you say?"

"But you must be careful not to—" Before she could finish, a fast-moving wave, very large, came up on their starboard bow as the wind gusted at the same time. Since the sail was angled tightly to catch the wind, the combination was enough to make the boat heel sharply. Caught by surprise and unable to dislodge Mitchell's tight grasp on the tiller, Danielle cried out.

Jim leaped, catlike, to grasp the tiller and bring it over by sheer force. A good part of the wave slapped them in their faces as it went by. Mitchell took the worst of it. He floundered in the stern, pushed from his seat by Jim. John appeared in the companionway, his frown changing to a deep laugh as he took in the situation.

Danielle was trilling with laughter, even as she exclaimed apologetically, "I'm so sorry, Mitch dear! I was just about to warn you, but—" She broke off and offered her hand to help him up.

Waving away the aid, Mitchell levered himself into a standing position. His shirt was heavily soaked with salt water, and drops of moisture hung from his chin and nose. He reached up to wipe the wetness away. A discomfited grin replaced the look of consternation on his face. "Sorry about that. I'll leave the sailing to someone who won't land us at the bottom of the sea. Jim's the expert here, not me."

The incident set the pattern for the day. Jim was truly in his element on the water. All his landbound awkwardness disappeared, and along with it any introverted tendencies he possessed. He went out of his way to teach Kathryn about sailing and even expounded on sea lore with a knowledge that had the Beresfords hanging on his every word.

Jim insisted on Kathryn's joining him at the tiller. "It's not that hard," he said. "The wind's steady now, and John's controlling the angle of the sails. Give it a try."

Kathryn glanced at Mitchell. His good humor was beginning to show cracks. She thought he was as amazed as she at the change in Jim, and rather disconcerted. Mitch was accustomed to being the leader, not the follower. But today Jim was in his element, and Mitch couldn't match him for experience.

"I don't know, Jim," she said tentatively. "I'll probably end up in the scuppers like Mitchell." Her conciliatory smile at Mitch was not returned.

"No, look, I'll show you," Jim said earnestly, putting his arm around her and placing her hands where they should go on the tiller. "Feel the response of the boat when you press like this?" In his eagerness, he leaned close beside her, his cheek pressing against her hair as he stared upward at the angle of the sail. His hands on hers made a minute adjustment to the tiller.

Absorbed in trying to see and feel what he meant, Kathryn forgot Mitchell's presence. Danielle had gone below, and John was stretched along the side of the upper deck, his eyes closed. For a moment, Kathryn could feel as though she were entirely in charge. There was the singing hiss of the hull through the water, the alive response from the tiller in her hands, and the virtual silence of their swift passage. Her teeth flashed white in a shining smile.

"You see what I mean, don't you?"

"Oh, yes. I could get drunk on it," she laughed. Her gaze fell on Mitchell, sitting ominously still on the other side of the cockpit. He wore a fierce scowl. Surely he couldn't be jealous. Not of Jim!

John sat up. "Not far now," he called over to them. "We should get to the island in about twenty minutes with this wind behind us."

Some fancy tacking and maneuvering brought the *BelleFemme* to anchorage. John and Jim lowered the dinghy over the side while Danielle directed Mitchell to bring the lunch hamper up from the tiny galley.

"I'm glad there's something I know how to do," he muttered, then laughed sheepishly when Danielle poked him in the ribs.

"You know how to eat, don't you?" she teased. "At least John isn't making us fish for our meal, as he sometimes does. This time we have it all prepared: lobster and beer."

An hour later, replete with the delicacies from the capacious hamper, the party took up various positions along the beach. John unrolled a chart he had brought from the yacht, and he and Jim began discussing tides and currents and coastal hazards. Danielle arranged herself on a blanket and cushion and advised Mitchell and Kathryn to do the same.

"I always find a short nap pleasant after a good morning's sailing," she said, opening a container of sun lotion and carefully anointing her face and throat before leaning back on the cushion.

Mitchell had been watching Kathryn through half-closed eyes as she repacked some of the lunch utensils. As she was about to join her hostess, he grabbed her hand.

"Kathryn and I are going to explore the island. You don't mind, do you?"

Danielle's gaze went from one to the other, and she smiled graciously, her eyes twinkling. "What a thing it is to be so young and vigorous. Certainly you should explore this charming little island." As Mitch tugged Kathryn along with him, she called, "Be sure to see the rock cove on the northwest corner!"

The rock cove was tiny, perfect and private. They found it after fifteen minutes of climbing over the hummocks, boulders, and fallen trees scattered along the mostly granite shore. Sheltered from the strongest breezes, the intimate cove had a small strip of coarse sand encircled by boulders and shrubs. Waves washed in and retreated with a rushing sound. Kathryn and Mitch dropped to the sand, panting from their exertion.

After a few moments Mitchell rolled over to where Kathryn was lying on her back, her eyes closed against the sun's rays. Leaning on his elbows, he stared down into her face until her lashes swept upwards. She looked up at him, her eyes wide and questioning, waiting.

"You're getting to me, you know," he said conversationally. Idly he reached for the crystal daisy that adorned the end of a braid. "You're such a contradiction. Look at these silly little things."

He pulled and the decoration came free in his hands. "I know you're a full-grown woman, twenty-four years old, according to your file. But sometimes you look so innocent I'd feel like a heel to even think of trying anything with you."

"Why, Mitchell, I do believe you have a conscience." She opened her eyes to their widest and treated him to her most saintly look.

"Why, Mitchell," he mimicked. "That's what I mean. Why don't you come out from behind that blue-eyed smoke screen and let me see the real you?"

She batted the blue eyes at him. "This is the real me—freckles and all."

"I give up," he said with mock resignation. "I'll just have to find out for myself."

He pulled the tie of her hat scarf. It came loose and he removed the hat, sliding his hands into her hair.

"I sunburn," she whispered in protest, her eyes caught and held in the green depths of his.

"I'll shelter you," he replied, his lips covering hers.

He tasted salty. She brought her hands up to clasp his head, her lips softening and parting as the kiss of exploration aroused sweet sensations. How incredibly dear he felt to her as her hands cradled him. She felt the thudding of his heart against her breasts, felt the warmth of him as his body moved more fully over her, supple and alive. Excitement began to sing in her veins.

"Kathryn, Kathryn," he murmured, brushing her face with lips that had gone soft and tender. She felt his delicate touch on her half-closed eyelashes, on her nose, and around the sensitive parts of her ear. The sound of the sea was muted by the thundering of her blood.

Mitch, darling, she cried silently. Amazement flooded her at the realization that the last of her defenses had been breeched and what remained behind them was love. She felt overwhelmed, lifted above her very sensible fears and doubts about him as a man. How could she possibly . . . No, how could she possibly not! In spite of everything, there was a sense of rightness in being in his arms like this. She wanted to tell him, but she was afraid. She could only show him silently.

A groan escaped Mitchell's throat as her hands found

their way under his shirt and slid up his naked back. He shuddered as she traced his spine with her fingers, letting his response guide her touch.

"Kathryn." His voice cracked on the husky word. "You're playing with fire. We're both playing with fire."

"Yes," she agreed, the word hardly audible.

He raised himself on his elbows, framing her flushed face with his hands, examining the eyes blue-hazed with passion. There was a tender satisfaction in his smile. "Whatever it is between us, it's something out of the ordinary. You know that, don't you?"

Uneasiness stirred deep within her. Her smile was uneven. "Yes, I know that. Are you sorry?"

He responded with raised eyebrows and an incredulous smile. "Oh, no. Whatever else I am, I'm not sorry."

"I thought you might not appreciate the distraction. You're so single-minded about your company."

He looked down at her for a long moment, considering her words. "You have been a distraction. And, I admit, an aggravation." His finger on her lips stopped her response. "I hadn't counted on a bright, sexy redhead straight from the farm coming into my well-planned life and throwing me into a state where I don't know which end is up. Do you know I've felt like punching Jim in the nose at least twice today? And he didn't even notice, the idiot."

"That's because he wasn't doing anything to annoy you." She put her fingertip on his lower lip and ran it back and forth, lightly touching his teeth.

His teeth took her fingertip and held it prisoner. His eyes promised many things before they wandered to her loosened hair. He sat up, his eyes narrowing. "I've had to listen to Jim talk about your hair 'til I think my teeth will grind down to nubbins. It's been driving me crazy. I'd like to have a few memories of my own."

She stared up at him, enchanted by the determination on his face as he finished the job he'd begun on her braids. He buried his hands in the silky strands and kissed her long and passionately. Lying back on the sand, he eased her over him, his long legs shifting to fit her against him. Her hair fell about his face, enclosing them in a flame-tinged world as their mouths met and merged again and again.

His hands explored her spine through the thin gauze of her embroidered blouse, duplicating what she had done to him, sending new tensions rippling through her. Then, in one smooth movement, his hands slid lower to caress the round curves of her buttocks.

"Kathryn." His voice was muffled and strange as his mouth moved to the curve between her neck and shoulder. His hands tightened, and she felt the inner trembling of his body as though it were part of herself. "You know I want to make love to you. I've wanted to since that first week."

Trying to control her response to his evocative words, Kathryn raised her head and stared down into his slumbrous eyes. "Mitch, I . . ." She couldn't continue.

"I know you feel it, too. Your body speaks for you." He moved beneath her, only heightening her inability to say anything. But the time for words was past. With economy of motion, he reversed their positions, bringing her under him, molding her yielding form to his overwhelming maleness.

She felt his hands busy under her blouse as they released the front catch of her bra and pushed it away from the cushiony mounds of her breasts. Her breath caught, but she made no effort to protest.

He raised himself and stripped off his shirt, shoving it under her head as a pillow. When he lowered himself once again, he silently sought her breast through the gauzy blouse, the moistness of his mouth penetrating the barrier of the fabric.

Being in the small cove was like inhabiting a seashell, a world consisting only of the sound of the sea, the scent of their heated bodies, and the dreamlike sensations he was creating in both of them. Her fingers dug into his strong,

111

bare shoulders, and her breathing became small sounds that were not words but communication nevertheless, for a fine tremor passed over him as he heard them. The silken smoothness of his skin intoxicated her. She luxuriated in the freedom to touch him as he was touching her.

How they heard Jim's call from around the headland, Kathryn never knew. The call invaded the tiny pocket of privacy like an echo coming from inside herself.

"Hey, Mitch! Where are you?"

Mitchell was the first to come to his senses. His chest heaving, he sat up, staring rather wildly about him. As Jim called again, he grasped the situation and fumbled for his shirt.

"I'll go head him off," he said, his voice raw. He pulled the shirt over his head and emerged blinking, his eyes still dazed. When he had risen to his feet, he looked down at her and his eyes fell on the wet transparency of her blouse over her breast. The shape and color of her nipple was clearly discernible.

Still in a state of shock, Kathryn was aware of the effort it took him to tear his gaze away. She sat up as he turned away to move swiftly over the rocks. He glanced back once.

"Hurry up, Kathryn!" he called. "They'll be wanting to leave soon. It's getting late."

It hadn't been easy to ignore the Beresfords' curiosity or Jim's puzzled gaze. All in all, Kathryn wasn't sorry when they said good-bye to their host and hostess and headed for the car. Yawning mightily, Jim refused to let Kathryn sit in the back of the Mercedes, saying he was ready to catch a nap on the return trip. Mitchell frowned at her evasiveness.

"What is it?" he queried softly under cover of a romantic tune coming from the radio. "What bee has gotten under that Vermont bonnet of yours?"

The sun had disappeared long since, but its light had been slower to vanish. In the twilight before full dark,

Kathryn studied his profile. This was the man she loved. But a phrase came to mind—love without reservation. Hers was not a love without doubts.

"It's been a long day," she murmured.

"And a full one." It was amazing how much meaning he packed into the four words.

She cleared her throat, but no words came.

"Don't tell me my saucy farmer's daughter is speechless!"

"Some things are better not discussed," she replied, casting a quick glance toward the back seat, where Jim was dozing.

"The time and place can be better arranged, but the discussion has to take place."

"I'm not sure it should."

There was a silence that stretched out as the powerful car sped along the throughway. Then a low laugh came from her companion.

"It's too late, Kathryn. I think it was too late when you first walked into my office looking like butter wouldn't melt in your mouth. No wonder it took me so long to figure out the game you were playing—the farmer's daughter and the city slicker."

"Why, Mitchell, I don't know what you mean," she answered demurely, her hands folded in her lap.

"Oh, yes, you do. And it's high time we played a more sophisticated game." A strong-fingered hand reached out to cover her clasped ones, and she could not prevent herself from curling her fingers around his.

Awareness of what had happened that day crackled between them. Only Jim's presence prevented them from bringing out into the open what was paramount in both their minds. It hung unresolved, and Kathryn knew Mitchell wouldn't allow her to push it aside, to go back to where they'd been before that hour in the sandy cove. She wasn't even sure she could.

Mitchell broke the electric silence. "Unfortunately, I have to go out of town this week. Let's arrange for that discussion as soon as I get back. Better yet, I could drop Jim off first, and you could come home with me tonight. I've been wanting to show you my place."

She uncurled her fingers. "No, thanks. I'm tired and I just want to go home."

"That's fine with me, but that bed of yours doesn't look especially comfortable."

She forgot about Jim and raised her voice. "I wasn't inviting you to share it!"

"No? I thought—"

Jim's voice broke in mildly. "You don't have to worry about me, you know." His head appeared over the back seat. "You can drop me off at a bus stop and flip a coin."

Kathryn glared at the two of them. "You can drop *me* off first, and then you can both—"

"Kathryn." Mitch remonstrated.

"I really am tired, Mitchell," she said, pulling herself together. They had reached the city, and she welcomed the thought of taking refuge in her apartment to think things over. "Would you mind just dropping me off?"

After a moment during which he obviously struggled with the inclination to argue further, Mitchell did as she asked. Leaving the patient Jim in the car, he walked with her to her door. There, after she had opened the door and he had done a quick safety check, he leaned his forehead against hers, his arms clasping her loosely.

"You know I don't want to leave you tonight," he said, his lips warm against her heated skin.

"I need to think, Mitch," she pleaded softly. "What happened today was . . . almost too much. I can't quite . . ."

"I understand, darling. It was almost too much for me." His mouth twisted ruefully. "Given the circumstances, it was a dumb thing to start. But we'll have to finish it . . . sooner or later."

His arms tightened, and his mouth found hers, moving insistently, reminding her of the passion they had shared and left unsatisfied. After a long moment, Mitchell reluctantly released her.

"We'll talk when I get back, darling," he said, his voice low. A nerve twitched in his cheek. "It can be here or at my place, but it has to be."

Kathryn caught herself almost nodding in agreement. With a smile that tried to be noncommittal but looked poignantly unsteady, she stood on tip-toe and touched his lips in a final fleeting kiss.

"Good night, dear Mitchell. Thanks for a lovely day." She closed the door, leaving him on the other side. Her emotions were painfully confused as she did what she had done once before, listen to the sound of his footsteps as he walked away.

8

Kathryn was in the lobby watching Susan arrange some bronze chrysanthemums in a white vase. She'd missed her usual bus and had been caught in Monday morning traffic, so for once she wasn't early. "They remind me of autumn in Vermont," she said wistfully.

The elevator arrived, and her head swung up as Mitch walked out of it, looking healthy and handsome with his seagoing tan.

"Morning, Susan. That's a nice bunch of mums you have there." He turned to Kathryn, his eyes crinkling with humor. "And you, Ms. Lambert, have a lovely bunch of freckles."

Kathryn could feel her cheeks turn pink to match her sunburned nose. "*Most* of the time I had on a sun hat to protect myself," she retorted. From the corner of her eye she saw that Susan wasn't missing a single step of this tango between them, and she hurried toward the elevator. "I also have a bunch of work waiting for me."

Mitch winked at her just as the elevator doors closed.

An office romance certainly had its awkward moments, she thought with amusement as she settled down at her desk. She'd hardly begun working on the data bases when Jim paused in her doorway.

"What a beauty," he sighed.

Kathryn looked up, startled.

"I've dreamt about her for the last two nights."

"The *BelleFemme*," Kathryn correctly surmised, grinning.

"When I have my debts paid off, I'm going to trade in *Jargon* for something a little classier, I think."

"Debts?"

Jim finally focused on her face. "Yeah, well, you don't have a business crash without having a few debts lying around. It's okay, though. I borrowed from my parents, so I can take as long as I want to pay them off."

No wonder he still had that incredible car, she thought sadly. "Maybe the Beresfords will invite you sailing again."

Her effort at consolation was unnecessary. "Actually, I prefer sailing my own, meager as it is. Everybody has a different way of doing things."

A burst of laughter from the next cubicle surprised Kathryn. It was low-pitched and lively, not a sound she recognized. She looked questioningly up at Jim.

"Our documentation expert," he explained. "I'll introduce you to her."

He loped out and was back in a moment, followed by a thin woman with the warmest smile Kathryn had seen since she'd arrived in Boston. The newcomer had the same straight sandy hair as Jim, but hers was artfully styled to frame her narrow face.

"Rita Sweeney, Kathryn Lambert," Jim said.

The tall young woman offered her hand. "Hi, Kathryn. Looks like you're hard at work." The slightly nasal quality of her voice and the way she pronounced *hard* made it clear she was a native of Boston but did not travel in the same circles as the Beresfords. She sounded more like the Irish bus drivers Kathryn met on her daily commute.

Kathryn was immediately taken with the woman's down-to-earth quality. "Nice to meet you, Rita."

Jim, his duty done, turned toward the door. "Want to join us for an orientation session on the program, Kathryn?"

"Not unless you need me. I have too much work piled up."

It was the same answer she gave Mitchell when he asked her to have lunch with him—not because she didn't want to, but because he'd phrased the invitation in a rather suggestive way.

"I've had to change my plans for the West Coast trip. I'm leaving this afternoon instead of tomorrow, and I thought we might eat upstairs in the penthouse while I pack."

"It would be a great way to miss your plane," she added.

"I have no intention of missing my plane."

"We had no intention of getting carried away on that island either," she reminded him.

"Look, I'm going to be gone for a week. Couldn't we just say good-bye?"

"Here or in a restaurant. I wouldn't be comfortable disappearing upstairs with you in the middle of the day, dodging people as I slip into the elevator—or whatever arrangements you make."

A frown started between his brows. "I don't make arrangements, Kathryn."

"I'm sorry." They sat looking glumly at each other for a minute before Kathryn smiled and said, "It's a stand-off."

His face relaxed, and the familiar gleam returned to his eyes. "To a lovers' quarrel."

"Something like that."

"Come on," he said, surprising her with an affectionate smile. "I'll take you out to lunch."

In the noisy restaurant they sat at a narrow table, leaning toward each other, knees touching. Kathryn found it difficult to concentrate on his words as he was telling her about his trip. His hand clasped hers on the table, his thumb lightly stroking the sensitive skin between thumb and forefinger. She almost regretted that he hadn't pressed her to go to his apartment. The sweet touch of flesh on flesh seemed an appropriate parting gift to each other.

When her food came, she was hardly able to touch it. He met her eyes with a questioning look. "Are you all right?"

"Yes, fine." She offered a brief flash of smile. "Just a little . . . queasy inside."

He grinned and squeezed her fingers. "We should have gone to the penthouse."

Kathryn did not reply.

When they arrived back at the office, they rode up together in the elevator. As soon as the door had closed he swept her into a brief but ardent kiss, releasing her just as the doors opened again.

Breathless, she called back at him, "Have a good trip."

"I'd rather stay here," he muttered before the elevator whisked him up to the penthouse to finish his packing.

Kathryn didn't see him again before he left. The tension in her body gradually eased as she forced her attention onto her work. With Mitch away, she could devote some of her time to Jim's project, and she wasn't surprised when Rita appeared in her office, looking quite at home in her stocking feet. She carried a set of print-outs, which she handed to Kathryn.

"Could you make these corrections as soon as possible?"

Kathryn glanced over the red ink changes. "Sure. That's a lot of modification."

"We're trying to make it user-friendly. Jim doesn't have any objection." Rita cocked her head. "He's real easy to work with, isn't he?"

"Yes. He helped me find my niche here."

As she turned to leave, Rita asked casually, "Is he married?"

Kathryn laughed. "You wouldn't even ask that if you'd ever seen his apartment. No, he's single."

Rita's eyes were bright with curiosity. "You've been to his apartment?"

"Once." Kathryn grimaced. "I had to get him turned out decently for a social evening with some investors, and it was quite a task. He didn't even know he owned an ironing board."

"Sounds like a number of guys I've met in this business. But usually they're not as . . . considerate as he is." With an elaborate shrug, Rita disappeared out the door.

The office seemed different with Mitchell away. Kathryn missed the sense of his presence in the building and the possibility that he would appear at her side or have her join him in his office. She thought he might call her at home in the evenings from the West Coast, but no call came. During the next two days both Susan and Jim mentioned that they'd talked to him at work, but he'd never asked to speak to her apparently.

Well, it was business, she reminded herself. If he had questions about the information she'd given him, he'd ask to speak to her. Probably it was a good thing he didn't; it meant he was satisfied with her work. Kathryn knew that was rationalization. If he was as interested in her as he seemed to indicate when he was with her, why wouldn't he even bother to call her when he was away?

The doubts that plagued her were only partially alleviated when Jim remarked cheerfully one morning, "He's running his tail off out there. The last time I talked to him, he had to hang up right in the middle of an important discussion to take care of some other business. I'm beginning to wonder if he even gets to bed at night—he sounds so preoccupied."

"This is the biggest thing that's come along for him so far," Kathryn remarked diffidently. "It could really make Tech Plus."

"I know." Jim rubbed a hand along his chin, looking perplexed. "Did I forget to shave this morning?"

Kathryn nodded. She hadn't wanted to mention it.

"Feels like it." He dropped down on the chair beside hers and asked confidentially, "What do you think of Rita?"

"I like her."

"Yeah, so do I. She catches on real fast, and she works like a beaver." He became abstracted for a moment, staring out the window. "I was thinking of asking her to have lunch with me."

"Then do it," Kathryn prompted.

"No. I can't if I didn't shave." Jim smiled sadly at her and wandered off.

Kathryn ate her own lunch in the Public Garden, watching the flat-bottomed swan boats glide through the water. The paddle mechanism hidden under the swan's wings was worked by a young man who smiled across at her. She smiled back and gathered up the waste paper from her meal, remembering the picnic on the island. Was Mitch's motto "Out of sight, out of mind"? She trudged back to the office with a heavy heart.

As she approached the building, she saw Rita climb out of a red convertible. Kathryn did a double take when she realized that the driver was Roger Owens. He waved to her but she merely nodded in return. There was no point pretending to be friendly with someone who'd caused her so much trouble.

Rita caught up with her at the door. "Do you know Roger?" she asked.

"Yes, but I wish I didn't."

Rita chuckled. "I wouldn't want to know him either if I didn't work for him."

"You work for Roger? I thought Mitchell said he hired you last week."

"No, I'm part of what Roger likes to call his 'stable of experts.' He loans us out to various companies for exorbitant fees. Then he takes the cream and gives us the milk. But I like the setup, changing jobs and meeting new people all the time. It's a challenge."

Jim met them coming off the elevator. He'd obviously gotten hold of a razor since Kathryn had spoken to him. "I looked for you," he said to Rita, "but you'd already gone off to lunch, I guess. Did you go with Kathryn?"

"No, Roger Owens. One of the perks of working for him is that he takes us to lunch at really fancy places, trying to pump us for any information we learn on our jobs that might be helpful to him."

A look of shock descended on Jim's face; Kathryn was more successful in hiding hers. Rita gave a snort of laughter. "No one tells him anything, Jim. It's just a routine dance we go through. Roger can't get over looking for shortcuts."

"Why don't you just refuse to go?" Jim demanded, offended at this example of business ethics.

"Well, it's always a good meal," she said complacently, "and if he can't induce you to talk at lunch, then he invites you on the company sailboat." She turned to Kathryn. "It's a terrific sailboat. Of course, Roger writes the whole thing off as a business deduction."

"But do you talk when you go sailing?" Kathryn asked, worried.

"No. Roger's never figured out that he's too busy on the boat to put the screws on you." She shook her head wonderingly. "For a clever man he certainly has his blind spots."

Jim had lost all interest in industrial espionage. "What kind of boat is it?"

Kathryn excused herself and went back to work, but the information had disturbed her. It had seemed bad enough to hire someone through Roger, but surely it was foolhardy to hire someone who actually worked *for* him. What Mitch had feared was that Roger would try to lure

Jim away from Tech Plus, but Roger sounded more of a scoundrel than that.

Kathryn desperately wanted to believe that Rita was as honest and loyal as she looked, but how could anyone be sure? Rita's loyalty needn't necessarily be to Mitchell and Technology Plus. Her paycheck came from Roger Owens. As the documentation expert, she had access to every bit of information about the security program. What if Roger wasn't satisfied with headhunting? Maybe this time he was interested in pirating the program itself, the way Jim's business had been ruined.

It was all speculation. Kathryn pushed it to the back of her mind, promising herself she'd be alert but not overly suspicious. Rita didn't seem the type to fall in with Roger's nefarious plans, if indeed he had any. If anything, Rita seemed amused by her employer, willing only to use him to the extent he used her. Kathryn would have to get to know her a lot better to guess whether Rita would crack under any pressure Roger might bring to bear on her.

The familiar electricity crackled through the offices the morning Mitchell was to return. Kathryn went straight to her cubicle, feeling nervous and annoyed. He hadn't been in touch with her the whole time he'd been away. How was she supposed to greet him under those conditions?

Her phone rang a few minutes after she'd begun work. She almost upset her coffee cup in her quick snatch for it but managed to keep her voice cool as she answered.

"I've missed you," Mitch said.

"It's only been a week."

"The longest, busiest week of my life."

Kathryn frowned at the receiver. "I thought you might call or send me a post card."

"I would have, if there'd been a minute to spare. Every time I thought of us lying on that beach, it raised my blood pressure so high I had to concentrate like mad on security systems and silicon chips. Even then I wasn't so successful, since that reminded me of integrated circuits."

He'd surprised a laugh from her. Kathryn shrugged at the hopelessness of staying angry with him for long. "Was it successful—your trip?"

"Yes, but it's going to mean even more work for me here."

"Oh."

His voice became husky. "That doesn't mean we won't have time to get together."

Kathryn could feel a tremor run up her spine. "Wh-when?"

"Not today, unfortunately. I have commitments all day and a meeting this evening. How about lunch tomorrow?"

"Okay."

"And keep the evening open, too."

Kathryn felt the deep bass of the words curl through her. "Yes, I will."

But he canceled lunch the next day and found himself unable to come by in the evening. Kathryn counseled herself to patience. It wasn't that he didn't want to see her but that this was an impossibly busy time for him. On the third day after his return she worked late, hoping he'd find his way up to her cubicle after everyone had gone home. She hadn't seen him alone since he'd left, although his eyes seemed to bore into her each time they met in the office.

Kathryn heard the elevator stop at the second floor. From her work space she couldn't see the doors, but she could hear Mitchell's tread across the floor. He didn't come directly to her cubicle, but to Jim's office down the hall. She heard his exclamation of annoyance, and shortly afterward he appeared in her doorway.

"At least *you're* getting some work done," he grumbled, crossing his arms over his chest and leaning against the door frame. "I can't get anything accomplished with all these meetings. I have another one in half an hour. But I thought Jim would work late tonight. He usually does."

"He's gone sailing."

"It's hardly worth getting that little dinghy of his out for a sail before dark."

Kathryn shoved some papers aside on her desk. "He wanted to show Rita the *Jargon*."

His eyes instantly narrowed. "Why the hell would he want to do that?"

"Because they like each other," she said defensively.

"I'll bet." He stared out the window for a minute, thoughtful. "She's trying to get him to work for Roger."

"Nonsense. She doesn't even like Roger."

His lips twisted sardonically. "You're too trusting, Kathryn. If she didn't like him, she wouldn't work for him. Her skills would be invaluable to any number of people."

Kathryn rose to stand in front of him. "Roger's the one you have to look out for, Mitch, not Rita. He tries to pump all his people about the work they do for other companies."

He touched her face with one long finger, as though he'd just realized he was alone with her. "Roger's a headhunter, sweetheart, not a pirate." His lips curved with amusement. "You've suddenly become very protective of my business, haven't you?"

"I suppose so," she admitted grudgingly. "I'd like to make up for any trouble I've caused."

"There are lots better ways to do that than letting your imagination run away with you." He bent his head to capture her lips. The hunger that had obviously been tamped down for some time immediately became apparent in his kiss. His lips clung against hers, nibbling, tasting. He whispered her name with a hoarse urgency. "Let's go upstairs."

Kathryn was moved by his need and by her own eager

response. But her head was still clear enough to remember what he'd just said. "You have a meeting in half an hour."

He drew back, his glazed eyes quickly focusing on his watch. "Damn. Twenty-five minutes, and I have to change. Look, I'll call you later if I get a chance, okay?"

Kathryn nodded as she dropped down into the chair beside her desk. His smile was brief and sure of her. He was gone without another word, leaving her there to stare after him. Her heartbeat gradually slowed, and she forced herself onto her feet, determined to be out of the building before he left.

There was no call from him that night.

All day Friday he was gone from the office. Kathryn kept expecting him to appear at her door or to be on the line when the phone rang, but neither happened. When she went to the lounge to get coffee late in the afternoon, she found Jim and Rita there, deep in conversation. Rita smiled across at her, then arched her brows.

"Is something wrong? You look like you've lost your last friend."

"Oh, no, I'm just a little tired," Kathryn said.

Jim took her cup and filled it with coffee. "Working too hard," he informed her knowledgeably. "Everyone seems to have been struck by the bug. I tell you what, Kathryn. Rita and I are going out to dinner. Why don't you come with us?"

Rita looked a little surprised by this invitation. But her natural friendliness exerted itself to overcome Kathryn's protests. "It's just what you need," she assured her. "Some good food and friends to talk to. We're going to a family-style Italian restaurant I've been to. When Jim remembers to eat, his stomach seems to be a bottomless pit."

Probably Kathryn wouldn't have accepted their offer, except that she couldn't bear the thought of sitting around her apartment waiting for Mitchell to call—or not call. "Well, if you're sure." Her voice was still doubtful.

"It's settled," Jim said firmly. "We'll have a great time. I've been meaning to take you out again since that night we went to the Beresfords, only things have gotten so . . ." He shrugged, at a loss for words, but his gaze went to Rita.

"Yes, haven't they?" she agreed, her eyes twinkling. "We're leaving from work, Kathryn. If you can bear Jim's car . . ."

"Sure."

Kathryn was intent on getting her thoughts off Mitch's negligent treatment of her. Oh, she knew this was the most hectic time he'd ever gone through with his business, but that hardly eased her mind. It was sobering to watch his preoccupation with matters relating only to Technology Plus. How quickly he could stem the tide of his interest in her, even when flickers of passion had been stirred!

Kathryn couldn't believe his single-mindedness boded well for her—or for any other woman competing with his company. No wonder he'd never married! Who would agree to play second fiddle to a spreadsheet of profits and losses on computer software?

And yet, she couldn't help but study Jim and Rita. Surely if there was a man caught up in his work— actually, somewhere out in space a lot of the time—that man was Jim. As they ate dinner, his abstracted gaze rested on the table, but his thoughts were obviously far away. After Rita had asked twice if he'd like more wine, she shrugged at Kathryn and said, "We've lost him. He'll probably snap out of it in a minute."

"Doesn't it bother you?"

"Not really." She gave Kathryn a shrewd glance. "What good would it do if it bothered me? You can't change someone like Jim. If you can't take them the way you find them, then you don't take them at all."

Kathryn stared down at her hands. "Yes, I suppose you're right," she said softly. But was it the same thing,

Jim's absorption in his thoughts and Mitch's devotion to his company? The thought teased at her throughout the meal.

There was something endearing about Jim's awkward delight in Rita's company. It bore no resemblance to Mitch's smooth sophistication. But, for good or ill, it wasn't *Jim's* smile that made her heart hammer or *his* voice that sent a thrill through her nervous system. She sat silent in the back seat of the car on the way to her apartment, listening to her companions' easy talk.

"I'll wait in the car," Rita announced when Jim pulled up in front of the apartment building.

Kathryn and Jim pushed their way through the door into the lobby as she said, "I don't know why the door's always unlocked. It's not much of a deterrent to criminals, is it?" She smiled up at him and stood on tiptoe to kiss his cheek. "Thanks for taking me with you, Jim. I had a lovely time."

"Did you?" The voice issued from the shadows at the back of the lobby near her apartment door.

Kathryn jumped slightly in surprise, and Jim nodded to Mitch as his employer detached himself from the wall he was leaning against and walked toward them.

"Yes," Kathryn said, with all the firmness she could muster, "I did."

"Well, we were glad you could come along." Jim stuck out his hand and Mitch reluctantly shook it. "See you both Monday." And he walked away, whistling off key.

"I tried to call you," Mitchell informed her as she turned her back on him and approached her door.

"Wonders never cease."

"Kathryn, you knew this was going to be a tough week." There was a hard note in his voice. "It's not fair to use Jim to get back at me for being busy."

"I wouldn't think of using Jim. That's not one of the things I do—use people." She met his eyes with a hard stare of her own.

"And you think I do?"

"Sometimes I think you'd use anyone to make this security program pay off."

"Well, you're wrong." He tilted her chin up with one finger and frowned down at her. "You forget I have an office full of people who have to get a check each month. I'm responsible for them. If Tech Plus fell apart, they'd all be out on the street looking for jobs. I can't just let everything we've worked for go to pot on account of my personal involvement with you. That would be getting my priorities all out of whack."

"It looks to me like you always put your business interests before your personal ones."

His lips tightened for a moment, then he lifted his shoulders in a gesture of frustration. "You've seen it that way from the start, Kathryn, because that's the way you wanted to see it. Right from the day Nate took me to the farm, you were convinced I was a heartless businessman. For some reason that goaded you into challenging me. All I wanted to do was repay a debt, if I could."

She stood for a long moment, reading the truth of his words in his eyes. "It hurts me that you haven't made more of an effort to see me since you've been back. I've tried to understand, but it's been five days, Mitch."

"I know it's been too long. You have to believe that I've wanted to be with you every minute." He ran a hand distractedly through his hair. "But I can't put my personal pleasure above the needs of fifteen other people at a time like this." He grimaced slightly. "I would have, though, if I'd known you were going to go out with Jim."

"I had dinner with him and Rita. They only included me because I looked so forlorn at work this afternoon." She turned toward her door, searching for her keys in her purse. When she looked up again, she noticed a tall green box standing behind the wooden planter outside her door.

"You brought me flowers!"

"No, I sent them this afternoon, in case I couldn't get over here. When I called and there was no answer, I thought I'd just come over and wait for you."

Kathryn slipped the box open to expose a dozen long-stemmed roses, red and white, and a pristine card lying on them. She lifted the card and read: *Dear Beauty, Thank you for your understanding. The Beast*

With a grin she turned and unlocked the door. "My landlord doesn't allow pets," she confided, "but I'll sneak you in."

9

The roses stood triumphantly in the only container Kathryn could find for them, a milk carton. She and Mitchell sat on the sofa, staring at them, each waiting for the other to make the first move. Kathryn found that his nearness was affecting her as it always did. Her heart was pounding and her mouth ached for the touch of his lips. Their sparring had left her unsettled, but she realized suddenly that he had used it to keep his passion in check until she made the decision that was ultimately hers.

A thrill of anticipation shivered through her body, and she knew the decision had already been made. She reached out to touch his cheek, smiling against the remaining sternness in his eyes. "I'd rather be kissing you," she said softly.

"Would you?" There was an abrupt change in his expression, and his voice had become husky. The hands that had been clenched at his sides now opened, palms upward, and she placed hers in them. He rubbed his thumbs soothingly over her flesh, staring for a long moment into her eyes. "I couldn't bear for this to be another dead end, Kathryn."

"It isn't. There's a rainbow at the end of this road, Mitch," she whispered, her throat tight with tension.

"And a pot of gold?" he asked, smiling.

"One never knows until one hunts for it."

"I'm a very good hunter."

Kathryn wrinkled her nose. "I know you are."

His lips caught hers in a wild kiss that nearly took her breath away. And yet his hands, moving to her back, stroked in the slowest, most sensual circles over her shoulder blades and down to her waist, pressing her lightly to him with a different kind of urgency. Kathryn could feel her mouth tingle with the touch of his tongue, but the flesh on her back, too, came alive under the thin cotton top.

"You're delicious," he murmured.

"Farmers' daughters are particularly susceptible to flattery," she rejoined, running her hands over his muscular shoulders. Their faces were so close she could see the almost invisible freckles, and she tilted her head so she could run her lips softly across them. She could feel his hands hesitate on her back. "I love your freckles. They make you look more . . . human."

"What's that supposed to mean?" he demanded, his eyes twinkling.

"Oh, nothing much. It's just that otherwise you'd be too handsome to look wholesome."

"Entrepreneurs are susceptible to flattery, too."

His lips sought and found hers, nibbling them before his tongue slid into her mouth to explore the warm moistness of it. This was a lengthy exploration, now urgent, now slow and seductive. Time was not a factor, except in the steady mounting of sensation in her body. Kathryn found that she'd slid farther down on the sofa so that her body was ranged along his for its entire length. His heart beat against her chest like an echo of her own.

For long moments they lay that way, clinging to each other, until he brought one hand between them to glide gently over her breast. An immediate response flashed through her, tugging at her very depths. A sigh escaped into his mouth.

His lips moved to plant light kisses on her cheeks and nose and forehead; the backs of his fingers stroked the crest of her bosom, teasing the hidden nipple into prominence. With each stroke a cascade of longing surged through her.

"You don't need this shirt on," he murmured, tugging it out of her slacks and drawing it up over her head.

"It was the only thing protecting me from this nubby material," she protested, trying to catch her breath.

"I knew this scratchy sofa was going to be the ruination of me." He winked at her and drew her over on top of him, far enough up along his body that the lacy bra reached his chin. With one sure finger, he followed the curve of her breasts just under the gossamer fabric, his eyes on her face. "I suppose farmers' daughters always wear a bra," he said.

"Almost always."

His mouth followed the route of his finger and then slid down to capture one nipple and then the other through the fabric. Kathryn gasped from the exquisite sensation of it. Her hands came to hold his head toward her as her fingers played recklessly in his hair. The whole of her body felt soft and yearning against the lean urgency of his.

She drew back from him, her body trembling slightly. "I . . . I think maybe we should have a piece of cake now. There's one in the kitchen. I made it for when you came. I mean . . ." Kathryn nervously brushed back a strand of hair that had fallen forward on her cheek. "It's called Chocolate Decadence. Susan gave me the recipe for it."

Mitchell studied her face and then nodded. "Yes, I

think Chocolate Decadence is just what we need right now."

"Good!" Relieved, she bounced off the sofa, looking fleetingly at her shirt on the floor. Mitch shook his head and she shrugged, marching into the kitchen with her one long braid swinging sassily back and forth in front of him as he followed right behind her.

The dessert was in the refrigerator. When she bent to get it, he took a firm grip on her braid and began to unfasten the ribbon tied there in a bow. Kathryn turned to watch him do it, holding the cake against her chest. When the ribbon was off, he undid the elastic and tossed it toward the wastebasket.

"Hey, I save them," she protested.

"Not this one." His fingers were already working through the pleats of hair, loosening them so the full glory of the fiery tresses fell about her shoulders. "God, how I've wanted to do that," he sighed, his hands filled with masses of hair on either side of her face. "You have the most incredible hair."

"Yes. Well, thank you." His eyes were intent on her face and she swallowed hard. "We were going to have dessert."

"Yes, we were."

"Chocolate Decadence," she reminded him, feeling a bit unsteady.

"Of course."

Kathryn lifted the cake onto the counter and reached into a drawer for a knife. Mitchell stepped abruptly backwards, and she giggled at him. "It's for cutting the dessert."

"Of course," he agreed. "Why don't you let me do it?"

"Okay. Want a glass of milk with it?"

He looked startled. "Milk? Sure. Why not?"

Two glasses and two plates were quickly produced, and she poured the milk while he lifted slices of cake onto the plates. "Are we going to eat it with our fingers?" he asked.

Kathryn bit her lip. "No, of course not. I just forgot." She dug in a drawer for the forks.

"I wouldn't mind," he assured her. But he accepted the fork she offered and, instead of heading back to the living room, slid onto the counter and offered his hand to her.

Reluctant, Kathryn suggested, "We could go back to the sofa."

"I like this better."

She accepted his hand and found herself seated almost on top of him on the short countertop. He held a forkful of cake for her to sample. His eyes were glowing with humor—and something more. Kathryn found it difficult to swallow the cake. Even as he tried a bite himself, he kept his gaze on her.

"This is delicious," he said softly.

Before she realized what he intended, his lips were on hers again, warm, pressing. She heard the clatter of his plate as he set it down behind him, and felt the firmness of his hand at her breast again. The evening light was fading at the window behind the sink, but she could clearly see that his other hand had moved behind her.

The lacy bra was unhooked so quickly she made a small murmur of surprise, which was quickly silenced by his hungry mouth. There was no longer a wisp of fabric between her flesh and his hand. His thumb swept wide over her breast, caressing the sensitive skin, rubbing against the hardened nipple. Kathryn sat helplessly frozen, her plate in her hand, drinking in the erotic deluge that was sweeping over her.

His mouth left hers and traced its way to her chin and then her throat. He stopped just short of her breastbone and slid off the countertop to stand in front of her. The rumpled hair, the burning eyes, the generous mouth, all made her shiver with desire for him. The bra hung awkwardly at her elbows but she hardly noticed until he took her plate and set it aside, gliding the bra off and tossing it on top of the refrigerator.

"I'll never find it again," she laughed.

"Sure you will. Next time you go to get a glass of milk, it'll fall on you." Both of his hands moved up to cup her breasts, sending delicious tremors through her. The tips felt swollen and eagerly awaited his touch, but it was his mouth that covered one, taking it in, tasting it with his tongue, flicking and teasing it. Kathryn put her arms around his neck, holding him tightly against her, wishing this excitement could last forever.

"You're so beautiful," he whispered against her. "I could eat every one of these freckles."

"Why don't you eat your cake instead?" she suggested, somewhat breathless.

He grinned at her. "If you insist."

First he handed her her plate; then he retrieved his own. It was almost dark in the kitchen now, but neither bothered to turn on a light. Nor did he move away from his position in front of her. But his constant gaze, instead of making her feel uncomfortable, merely served to keep excitement rioting through her body, sped on by the knowledge that when the cake was finished . . .

He licked the last morsel from his fork and set the plate carefully on the counter. Kathryn wasn't quite finished with hers, so he took the fork from her nerveless fingers and fed her the last two bites. His other hand was at her waist, the thumb stroking above and below her slacks. When he had disposed of the second plate, he carefully unfastened the button and slid down the zipper. Then he pulled her into his arms, holding her easily above the floor, pressed against him. His mouth clung to hers and her full breasts strained against the soft fabric of his shirt.

As he lowered her to the floor, he worked the slacks down over her buttocks, and they slid to the linoleum with a soft swish. Now she could feel the texture of his pants against her naked legs and the hardness of his desire against her torso. Kathryn's mind had ceased operating on its usual wavelength. Explosive emotions were coursing through her, taking over every fiber of her being, until she felt only the need for their joining.

They stood tightly holding to one another for a long time, the only sound in the room the hum of the old refrigerator. His hands played over the smooth fabric of her underpants, pressing her rhythmically to him until she was in an agony of longing. With his tongue he circled her lips once again, then took her hand and drew her toward the bedroom.

"My nightgown," she mumbled inanely, suddenly feeling a tremor of hesitancy as he hurried her along. She pulled her hand free and scooted into the bathroom, where she would have closed the door on him if he hadn't already managed to step in behind her and flick on the light. He was grinning at her.

"You won't need it, lovey."

"Well, I just thought . . ." She swung away from him and pulled the nightgown down from its hook on the door, clasping it to her chest. In the mirror she caught sight of herself, her hair wildly disarrayed, her eyes wide with a variety of conflicting emotions. "Oh, heaven!"

"Yes, heaven," he agreed, his eyes twinkling. "Where's your hairbrush?"

Kathryn blinked at him in astonishment. He reached around her for the brush, which was lying on the sill above the sink. "Turn around," he said. Kathryn did as he ordered, and he started brushing her thick, fiery hair with long, slow strokes. She watched his face in the mirror, concentrating on the small, amazingly seductive task. No one had brushed her hair since she was a child, and it astonished her to see what pleasure he got from doing it.

When her hair glowed in the bright light, he set the brush down and turned her toward him. "Everything about you is radiant, Kathryn." His voice was husky. He gently extracted the nightgown from her clenched hands and flung it over the shower curtain rod, exposing her breasts once again. "Everything," he said, touching the tips of them with his thumbs.

The chaos in her was instant. But his hands did not remain at her chest. Instead they wandered slowly down toward her last remaining item of apparel. As his lips met hers, his fingers slid beneath the silky cloth, and a new, more powerful wave of urgency swept over her. She murmured her pleasure against his mouth. Her tongue circled the firmness of his lips and strayed into the tender recesses beyond. Unbidden, her body arched toward him, insistent with desire.

"Oh, Kathryn," he moaned, drawing back.

"Yes," she whispered. Without another word she slipped past him, into the hall and the bedroom beyond.

Mitchell followed her, looking dazed. He had already begun to unbutton his shirt. Kathryn climbed onto the bed as he discarded the shirt and unzipped his slacks. The light from the bathroom outlined him in the dark room and cast a shadow that reached all the way to where she lay. He looked like a giant standing there, magnificent in his nakedness.

"Is this a safe time for you?" he asked. "I don't want you to have that worry on your mind. I've brought—"

"No, I'm fine. Thank you."

His shadow engulfed her before he reached the bed. As he stood over her, blocking the rectangle of light through the doorway, she reached up and clasped his hand. "I'm a little nervous."

"You won't be," he promised softly, sitting down and running his hands over her shoulders, massaging them with firm, strong fingers. "I want to call up every ounce of pleasure your wonderful body has to offer. That's nothing to be nervous about. You're with me, Kathryn. We've been burning for each other for weeks now. This is where the flames take over."

Kathryn could feel the burning inside her. She ran her hands through the hair on his chest and down his sides to his waist. He was right, of course. From the moment they'd first seen each other, the attraction had been incredibly strong. Fighting against it had always been a losing battle. There was something about him that struck sparks in her, that had made her smolder with a physical yearning for far too long. Her hands sliding over his bare skin merely served to reinforce this truth. She felt a shiver of excitement run through her.

"Aren't you going to make room for me?" he teased, a finger following the line of her lips.

She scooted over on the mattress, and he eased himself down beside her, propping himself on one elbow so he could face her. The pale light coming through the door fell softly on her body and gleamed in her eyes. He studied her golden form, running his eyes over the length of her before he shook his head wonderingly and said, "You're a work of art, Kathryn. Beautiful and brimming with a freshness that's all too rare." His fingers began to trace a path over the silky flesh of her breasts, lingering at the tips to tempt a renewed hardness. And then his mouth came to cover one breast, and his hands moved down her body to caress the skin of her thighs.

An ache swelled in her, filling her to bursting, but he paused, letting the ache ebb ever so slightly. His mouth and tongue followed the path of his hands, building up the unbearable tension yet again, only to withdraw the stimulation a moment before the crest was reached. Kathryn could feel her breath come in ragged bursts, and her body trembled with the need for him. The whisper of a moan escaped her lips, and he smiled, above her now, murmuring her name as he entered her.

The slow, steady rhythm of their lovemaking now spun into a new pitch, fevered and demanding. Kathryn clung to his hard, warm back, her fingers working urgently against the solid strength of him. Flashes of fire shot through her, consuming every fiber, every thought, every feeling except pure delight. The ultimate physical pleasure captured her body and then his, draining her of tension, rewarding her with a feeling of amazing renewal —and a oneness with Mitch that thrilled and astonished her.

And frightened her, too, a little.

Flushed with release, she smiled shakily at his wide, satisfied grin. His hands were caught in her hair, stroking it gently back from her face. "You're a dream come true, Kathryn," he whispered, kissing her tenderly on the lips. "More than a rainbow. The whole pot of gold. Does a pot sound too prosaic? A chalice, perhaps."

"You're ridiculous," she laughed, hugging him to her. "I thought you were going to say a milkpail."

"Only a farmer's daughter would think of that," he chided, his eyes decidedly playful. "But then, maybe only a milkmaid could share in such exquisite abandon. You're a real treasure, my dear."

"Thank you, sir," she murmured sleepily. "You might have made a good farm boy, yourself."

Exhausted, replete, Kathryn fell asleep to the sound of his deep chuckle. She was not aware that he held her for a long time, gazing into her softened face, a very peculiar look in his eyes.

The next thing she was conscious of was sunlight flooding through the new curtains at the window. Her thought that it was going to be a lovely day was barely completed when she became aware of an arm about her waist . . . and that she was snuggled tightly against a warm body. Mitch's warm body. Her eyes flew open to find his still closed, his face relaxed in profound sleep.

Kathryn could tell by the light in the room that it wasn't early, and she twisted slightly away from him to crane her neck toward the clock on the bedside table. Ten-thirty! They must both have been tired indeed to sleep so late. Kathryn couldn't remember when last she'd awakened after nine in the morning.

Thinking she'd surprise him with a hearty breakfast, she started to slide out from under his arm. It tightened about her, and his morning-deep voice muttered, "Where are you going?"

"To fix breakfast," she retorted cheerfully. "It's late."

"Let's be fashionable and have brunch at noon. We can find something to while away the time until then."

Kathryn felt his hand move up to cup her breast, and all will to desert the warm bed left her. She turned her head to meet his gaze and found his eyes already alight with smoldering desire. "I suppose there's no hurry."

"I'm not sure I agree with that, but I'm prepared to convince you." He drew her toward him, planting a light kiss on her forehead before attaching his lips firmly to hers.

Already the hand at her breast was causing a distinct sensation to grow within her. How quickly she responded to his touch! The magic of it erased any logical thought she might have, creating only a need that burned until it was satisfied. She had just reached out to touch him when she heard the doorbell ring in the distance. Her hand froze and a small frown formed between her brows.

"Just ignore it," he suggested, his voice coaxing.

She didn't understand what caused her sudden alertness, but she said, "No, it might be something important." Without another word she drew back from his hold and slipped quickly out of the bed. As she crossed the room to the closet, the bell rang again. Hurriedly she drew a quilted robe on over her nakedness, and with one last look at his disapproving expression, ran from the room.

On her way to the door she noticed the blouse on the floor and scooped it up, stuffing it under a cushion on the sofa. When she opened the door the scant few inches it would go on the chain, she gasped in astonishment. "Nate! Amanda! What are you doing here?"

Before they could reply, she closed the door and released the chain, swinging it wide to let them come in. Her astonishment at their arrival was too great for a moment to allow for her thinking of Mitch in the bedroom. She clasped each of them in a tight hug, insisting—as a lump formed in the pit of her stomach—that she was delighted to see them. "You didn't let me know you were coming," she said, trying hard not to make it sound like an accusation.

"We tried." Amanda came briskly into the room. Her gaze moved quickly around her, taking in the nubby green sofa and the faded carpet and the few other pieces of furniture. "We only decided to come last evening, and there was no answer here before we left Vermont. By the time we got to our hotel, it was too late to call you."

Nate offered a conspiratorial wink. "You know what your aunt is, Kathryn. Once she decides to do something, there's no stopping her." He seemed to notice her bathrobe for the first time. "Are you just up? You didn't use to keep hours like that in the country."

"No," she agreed, "I didn't. Can I get you a cup of coffee?"

"Just what we need," Amanda admitted with a small sigh.

Kathryn had been too rattled at first to notice that there were lines of strain about her aunt's mouth. She knew Amanda too well to think this was from the relatively short journey they'd made. "Is something the matter?"

Nate hastily interposed a question. "Did you have trouble finding this place? It's a good location." When Kathryn turned a worried eye on him, he said, "Let's get that cup of coffee. I haven't had one yet this morning, and it makes me grumpy as a bear."

Deciding it would do no good to press the matter, Kathryn shrugged and walked into the kitchen. Too late she realized this was a big mistake. There were two glasses of milk, untouched, sitting on the countertop, and her slacks lying crumpled on the floor. Amanda and Nate were right behind her, so she bent quickly to retrieve the pants and casually toss them over the back of the stool. She had every intention of brazening out this visit.

"A waste of good milk," her aunt commented, "but then, you probably don't get particularly good milk here."

Kathryn would have laughed at this chauvinistic remark, if her eye hadn't at that moment fallen on her bra. It hung down from the top of the refrigerator, one lacy cup covering the manufacturer's trademark on the door. She tried to divert her aunt's attention, forgetting that her uncle, too, had come as far as the entrance.

"I have two kinds of coffee," she chirped. "One's decaffeinated. People in Boston seem very concerned about how much caffeine they get, you know. Everywhere you go, they offer you a choice. Personally, I can't really tell the difference, but some people can. Which would you like?"

"Doesn't matter," Amanda said.

Kathryn turned to get her uncle's opinion . . . and found him staring straight at the bra. "How did that get there?" he demanded.

She hastily tweaked it off the refrigerator and mashed it up in a ball in her hand, wishing desperately that she could simply toss it in the wastepaper basket. "Well, I . . . I don't quite . . ." Stuffing it in the pocket of her robe, she attempted to ignore the question. "I could make us some pancakes if you haven't had breakfast."

There was silence in the room. Both her relatives were staring at her, their faces caught in that strange combination of disbelief and the horrified dawning of suspicion. Just then the toilet flushed in the distance. Kathryn colored to the roots of her hair.

"There's someone here," Nate announced, as though this were a fact of which no one else would be aware.

"Yes," Kathryn admitted. She grabbed the coffee pot and began to fill it with water. "I'll just be a minute getting this coffee."

"And I'll just be a minute seeing who it is!"

When he headed in the direction of the bathroom, Kathryn slammed down the pot and rushed over to him, grabbing his arm. "There's no need to do that, Nate. I'm sure he'll be joining us in a moment." Why couldn't Mitch have stayed in bed and slept until they left, or until she'd managed to get them out of the apartment? Her irritation with him, or perhaps with herself, was growing stronger as this farce continued unabated.

"Who is it?" Amanda asked, her voice grating with disapproval.

There was no need for Kathryn to answer. Already she could hear Mitch's footsteps in the short hall. She saw the stunned look on Nate's face just as she heard Mitch's voice. "Good morning, Nate. I didn't expect to see you in Boston."

"Apparently not," Nate growled. "Just what is the meaning of this?"

It was too much for Kathryn. Torn between a desire to laugh and cry, she stomped her foot and cried, "Will you all stop this ridiculous melodrama? I'm a grown woman. If I want to have a man spend the night, it's perfectly all right."

Mitch gave her a quelling look and offered his hand to Nate, who reluctantly took it. But there was a look in her uncle's eyes that Kathryn had rarely seen there. He was disappointed, hurt perhaps, and she couldn't tell whether it was with Mitch or herself. Amanda's lips were pursed in a tight pucker, as though she'd bitten into a lemon all unsuspecting. When Mitchell turned to her, she walked across the kitchen away from him, tossing back over her shoulder, "I wouldn't have thought to find you here, Mr. Grant."

"No, I imagine not. Kathryn would have been reluctant to write to you about us because of her working for me." His tone was smooth and confident. He moved to stand beside Kathryn, and his arm went possessively around her waist.

The coffee canister was in Amanda's hand by now, and she turned slowly to study the young couple. "What should she have written about you?" she asked with her usual bluntness.

"That we've become very attached to one another. This isn't a casual thing with us."

Kathryn's eyes flew to his face. How could he say such a thing to her aunt and uncle? Not that it wasn't true on *her* part. But his? Obviously he was just trying to save face for her. "I'm going to make pancakes," she announced.

"I'll help you," he said, all solicitous.

"Thank you, but I don't need any help. And the kitchen's too small for more than one person to work in. Why don't all of you go into the living room? Will you have pancakes?" she asked, turning first to her aunt and then her uncle. Amanda gave a brief nod; Nate muttered a yes. They followed Mitch into the living room.

Kathryn expected a vast silence from their direction, but was surprised almost immediately by Mitch's easy conversation. It took him very little time to have Nate and Amanda responding to his interested questions about the dairy farm and the weather conditions in Vermont.

As she worked diligently in the kitchen with her limited supplies, she felt a hardness developing in her toward Mitch. He was too smooth, too sure of himself. The ease with which he defused the situation did not make her proud of him. On the contrary, she considered it just another example of his careless sophistication, his certainty that he could handle any situation and turn it to his advantage. She didn't regret that she'd made love with him the previous night. How could she regret such bliss? She flipped one of the pancakes with an excess of frustrated energy. It couldn't go on.

The knowledge saddened her. She had to bite her lip hard to keep the tears that threatened from springing to her eyes. From a drawer she grabbed a paper napkin and blew her nose, hard and loud, before finishing her cooking. She'd have to quit her job, of course. It would be impossible to be near him every day and not have a recurrence of last night's indulgence. There would be other jobs, she consoled herself. Or she could go back to the farm.

"You can help me now," she called to Mitch as she stacked hotcakes on plates and set out syrup and butter. The coffee had finished perking, and she busied herself pouring it as he came into the room. From the corner of her eye she saw him sling plates along his arms like some glorified waiter. "You'll drop them," she couldn't help protesting.

"Bet?" There was a wicked sparkle in his eyes.

"No."

"Too bad. You'd lose, and that might be fun." He blew her a kiss and trotted out of the room.

Kathryn followed more slowly with the cups of coffee, setting everything down on the table in front of the sofa. Her aunt and uncle seemed much more relaxed, smiling at her.

"Those look great," Nate said heartily.

Mitch kept the conversation rolling while they ate. He offered office anecdotes and a modified version of their sailing excursion. Though his gaze was frequently on her, Kathryn refused to meet his eyes. She was unable to do justice to the food and finally pushed her plate away from her and sat back to sip at her coffee. Only when she again noticed the strain lines around Amanda's mouth did she remember her previous alarm.

"Why did you come?" she asked, interrupting the conclusion of one of Mitch's stories. He looked startled, but did not attempt to regain the floor. No one answered Kathryn, so she said, "Please tell me the truth. Something's wrong, isn't it?"

Nate made a negative gesture with one large hand, but Amanda nodded. Neither of them said anything.

"Well, tell me," Kathryn pleaded.

"Just tests," Nate grumbled.

Amanda was more forthcoming. "His doctor found a

tumor. Said the quickest way to find out whether or not it's benign was to have some tests done here at the hospital. We've just been there."

Kathryn held her breath, but Amanda was digging in her purse for a handkerchief. Nate laid a big paw on her shoulder and said, "Now, 'Manda. No use in carrying on. You'll frighten the girl."

"It . . . it wasn't benign?" Kathryn asked, frightened.

"We don't know yet. They'll call us at the farm later today or in the morning." He turned to pat her hand. "Now don't you be worrying about it. One emotionally overwrought female is more than enough."

Amanda trumpeted into her handkerchief and glared at him. Kathryn let out her breath and asked, "What would happen if it weren't benign?"

"An operation." A look passed between Nate and his wife, but neither expanded on the topic.

Mitch joined the conversation again. "So you're going back to the farm to wait for news?"

"Yes." Amanda straightened her shoulders. "No sense in hanging around town. Nate has things to do at the farm."

"I'll come with you," Kathryn said firmly.

"No such thing." Nate glanced briefly at Mitch and back at his niece. "There's no sense in your coming to the farm. If the word's good, we'll give you a call. If it's bad, well, I'll be back in town in a few days for an operation, and I can see you then."

"I want to come."

"Then I'll take you." Mitch set his coffee cup down and rose from his chair. "I'll get the dishes cleared away while you pack a few things. We can stop at my place on the way."

"No, no," Kathryn protested. "I can go with Nate and Amanda."

"How would you get back after the weekend?" he asked, sounding terribly reasonable. "I can stay at that little bed and breakfast place I noticed in town."

"You'll stay with us," Amanda assured him. "There's plenty of room."

Kathryn wanted to insist that Mitchell wasn't going at all, but it didn't seem fair to argue the point in front of her already beleaguered relatives. When they'd left, she'd have time to explain, and then she could rent a car and drive herself. Even if she decided she wanted to stay in Vermont, she'd have to come back to close up the apartment. And Amanda could stay there with her if Nate had to go into the hospital.

"All right," she agreed. It was difficult to avoid the piercing look Mitch gave her, but she covered her confusion by gathering together the empty dishes.

Amanda had already risen, determination straightening her back and forcing a smile to her drawn face. "Then we'll be off, dear, since we'll see you in such a short time. Nate's anxious to get back to the farm. Claudia's about to calf."

When she'd closed the door behind them, Kathryn leaned against it, eyeing Mitch warily. "Please don't suggest going back to bed."

He frowned at her. "It wasn't on my mind. I know you're worried about him, Kathryn. It won't take us long to get on the road."

"I don't want you to come."

"Why not?" The words were rapped out in hard staccato.

"Because this was all a mistake." She motioned vaguely toward the bedroom.

"You know it wasn't."

"But it was." She walked slowly away from the door, keeping a good distance between them. "I don't want it to happen again—ever. You're not the right kind of man for me to get involved with."

Mitch misunderstood. When he spoke, it was in a soft, coaxing tone. "They'll get used to the idea, honey. It was just the shock, walking in like that, unprepared. I think they realize now that it wasn't some Victorian seduction.

If they hadn't been under such a strain, they'd have known you're much too resourceful to be maneuvered into a one night stand."

"That's just what it was. There won't be any repeat, Mitch."

"What are you talking about?" he demanded, anger snapping in his eyes. "We have a future, Kathryn. Don't try to tell me you go in for that sort of thing, because I won't believe you."

One of the half-filled cups dropped from her hand onto the carpet. "Oh, God!" she muttered, falling to her knees to wipe at the soggy spot with a handful of paper napkins.

"Leave the damn carpet alone!" He stalked over to her and dragged her to her feet. "No one would notice if you poured syrup over the whole ugly thing and ground pancakes into it. I want an answer!"

Kathryn shrugged out of his grip and threw herself on the sofa, her arms crossed over her chest. "Then I'll give you an answer, Mitch. I got involved with a man like you when I was in college, and I refuse to do it again. He was very smooth, and bright, and totally self-centered. Worse, actually. He was ruthless where his career was concerned. His ambition was the only thing that counted. I might have made a nice ornament if I had been willing to take the scraps he could manage to toss me. Well, I wasn't . . . and I'm not going to be with you either. Don't think I regret last night. I don't. But I'm not going to let that happen again."

"What makes you think I'm like this jerk you're talking about? I can't see any resemblance at all."

"Of course you can't. But I can see it. I've been able to see it since the day we met." She shrugged her shoulders helplessly. "I don't want it to be that way, Mitch. Off and on I've tried to believe you really weren't like that. It just won't work. Believe me."

"I don't believe you." He ran a hand distractedly through his hair. "Kathryn, you're important to me. This isn't some little fling. I've had to spend a lot of time on business recently, it's true, but this is an important program we're working on and time is of the essence. If I've ignored you, I'm sorry. It won't happen again."

Kathryn slumped back on the sofa and looked up at him with sad eyes. She shook her head. "No, you're wrong. It would happen again and again. I couldn't stand it. Please go home now, Mitch."

"I'm taking you to Vermont."

"No."

Anger made his voice husky. "Don't be an idiot, Kathryn. This is no time to give your Uncle Nate cause to worry about you; he has enough on his plate. We told him I'd be bringing you, and under the circumstances, I'm damn well going to do it. If you want to hide your head in the sand after this is all sorted out, then do it—with my blessing! But I'm taking you to Vermont, so you'd better accept that and start packing."

Kathryn sat undecided for several minutes. There was enough truth to what he said to win her over, though, and eventually she nodded. "Okay. I'll pack, but only with the understanding that what happened last night is in the past."

"Of course it's in the past. Start packing, Kathryn. I'll take care of the dishes."

His answer was not wholly satisfactory, but she was too upset to argue with him. She went to the bedroom to pack.

10

~~∽∞∞∞∞∞∞∞∞∞∞∞~~

More cobbler, Jack?"

Amanda's dry, courteous voice revealed nothing of her anxiety for her husband. She had invited the rest of the Lambert family over for supper, treating the weekend as special only in that it was Kathryn's first visit since her move to Boston. They were all seated around the big dining table after enjoying fried chicken and all the trimmings.

Kathryn's brother-in-law Jack held out his plate for another helping of the peach cobbler that was fast being emptied from its dish. "Thanks," he said before turning to his wife. "Margaret, you should get the recipe for this from your aunt. Yours isn't nearly as good."

Margaret, a slightly older version of Kathryn, except that her hair was brown and her eyes a paler blue, glanced at her husband's rounded contours and down at her plate. "Yes, I'll do that. It's delicious, Amanda."

There was nothing new about the scene, Kathryn

realized, except in the way she saw it. She caught Mitchell's eyes on her, but she refused to meet them. When had Margaret changed from the sparkling young woman she'd been into this colorless matron? Her sister's hair was attractively arranged, and she wore a bright summer dress, but there was no enthusiasm in her. Kathryn wanted to believe it was Mitchell's presence that subdued her, and sought a way to show her sister to advantage.

"Margaret makes the most wonderful stained glass panels, Mitch," she said, smiling at Margaret. "There's one over the door at my folks' house and one in the kitchen here. I'll show that one to you later. What are you working on now, Margaret?"

Some animation did appear in her sister's eyes. "I've got a commission from the Grange to do a harvest scene. Everything's all drawn up, and I have the lead channels, but I'm waiting for the colored glass to arrive. I wish there were some place close enough to get it, instead of having to wait for the mail."

Jack grinned across at Mitchell. "You'd think three kids would keep her busy enough, wouldn't you? But no, she has to dabble in this artsy stuff. I'm not saying the panels aren't beautiful, you understand. Everyone says they are. But she hardly makes a cent, when all the expenses are taken into account, and having all that glass around the house is dangerous for the kids."

"I keep it locked up," Margaret protested, frowning at him. "And I only work on it at night when the kids are in bed."

"Georgie cut his finger on some just the other night," he went on imperturbably. "Came out for a glass of water, and Margaret was so wrapped up in what she was doing, she didn't notice him."

Kathryn glanced down at the three-year-old sitting on her left. There was no band-aid on any finger. She retrieved an oversize chunk of peach from his fork and cut it into small bites. "Tell me what you need, Margaret, and I'll find it for you in Boston. There must be stores there that sell the right supplies."

Her sister offered a grateful smile. "Thanks, Kat. I'd appreciate it."

Nate put down his napkin and rose from the table. "Let's have our coffee out on the verandah."

They all rose and distributed themselves according to the traditional pattern. Mitchell smiled at Kathryn and with a "when in Rome" look, followed the men outside. Amanda and Kathryn's mother started the washing up while Kathryn and Margaret carried in the dishes from the dining room. Noting the set of Amanda's mouth and her tired eyes, Kathryn gently untied the apron from her aunt's waist.

"You two go on out. Margaret and I can finish the dishes." Forestalling the older women's protests, she picked up little Trevor from the floor, where he was busy exploring the contents of a cupboard and handed him to his grandmother. "You'll be doing us a favor if you keep the imps out from underfoot."

When they were alone, Margaret avoided meeting Kathryn's eyes, busying herself with a dish towel. She was drying one of the large china plates when she remarked, "He doesn't really understand, you know. For him the farm and the kids and I are enough. And that's fine. I've tried to point out that lots of women do quilting, and that there's not much difference between that and stained glass."

"Of course not," Kathryn agreed stoutly, adjusting the apron over her shirtwaist dress. When she'd come downstairs in it, with her braids done up neatly and no makeup, Mitchell had eyed her quizzically.

"And it's true I don't make much money at it," Margaret went on. "Enough to cover the supplies, but hardly a decent wage for the hours I put in. That doesn't bother me. I like doing it."

"I'm going to have you do a panel for my apartment. You could make it look like a garden, to block out the weed patch I see every morning."

"Is it nice, your apartment?"

Kathryn giggled. "Not really. It's small and has ugly furniture, but I'm trying to make it livable."

"How about your job? Mr. Grant seems very nice."

"We've had our set-tos," Kathryn admitted, somehow not willing to share the deeper nature of the attachment with her sister at this point. "I like the work, though. At first there didn't seem to be anything for me to do but fill in around the place. Now I'm learning to do data-base management, and I feel more useful."

Margaret shook her head. "I don't even know what that is, data-base management."

"It's like setting up a filing system, only it's electronic, and you can do a lot more with it than with a bunch of papers."

"That sounds interesting," Margaret said wistfully. "And living in Boston. I've always wanted to live in Boston."

"Have you?" Kathryn was genuinely surprised. "I'm getting to like it, but I still sometimes long for the farm."

"Yes, but you can come here when you want, for weekends and vacations." She added another dry plate to the stack and shrugged. "I haven't been to Boston since Alice was born."

"Then you'll come and visit me one weekend," Kathryn declared firmly.

"What would I do with the kids?"

"Bring them. Or have Jack take care of them."

"I don't think he'd do that."

Kathryn looked over in surprise. "Why not?" But she could tell from her sister's face that Margaret didn't want to discuss it, so she hurried on. "Well, Mom wouldn't mind doing it. You'll be able to see my place and measure for a stained glass panel and get any supplies you need."

"Sure," Margaret agreed, but she didn't sound hopeful. "Maybe we can arrange it some time. Did Mom tell you who Tom Wells is seeing these days?"

During the long evening Kathryn's parents dropped remarks to the effect that she should consider returning to Vermont permanently. Margaret quietly supported Kathryn's choice to see what Boston had to offer, but her husband laughed at the idea that someone raised on a farm could be happy in what he called "that jungle." Nate and Amanda, having chosen not to inform the family of Nate's problem, tried hard to appear their ordinary selves, but Kathryn could see their strain.

It was Mitchell who made the effort to fill in the uncharacteristic periods of silence. He told them tales of California and Boston, relating anecdotes of the piratical side of computer technology that had all the elements of a mystery thriller, without the corpses.

Even Jack was caught up in the entrancing stories. As he left, a sleeping Georgie draped over one shoulder, he shook Mitchell's hand and said, "I guess if Kathryn's going to work in the city, she's lucky to work for you." Margaret pressed her hand silently.

When Nate and Amanda had walked off down to the cars with their guests, leaving Mitchell and Kathryn alone on the verandah, he turned to her and asked, "Would you like to go for a walk?"

Kathryn shook her head. "I'm confused . . . and exhausted. Tomorrow maybe." She touched his face softly with her fingertips before turning abruptly away from him and hurrying inside.

In bed she lay for a long time staring at the ceiling. Her body ached with a desire to join him in the guest room down the hall, where she might forget her doubts in his arms. But she wouldn't do that in Nate and Amanda's house . . . and she knew she shouldn't do it at all, if she couldn't settle the matter in her mind.

There was more than physical desire in her attachment to him. Kathryn refused to fool herself about that. She did love him, more strongly that she would ever have believed possible. Being on her guard against the negative aspects of his character hadn't seemed to protect her in the least. His amazing charisma, his ability and humor, his careless charm—all of them drew her to him with such potency she found it difficult to maintain the distance her mind cautioned.

If she continued to see him, wouldn't she just fall more hopelessly in love with him? While she enjoyed a few weeks, a few months in his exciting company, wouldn't he be getting restless and bored? Mitchell was not bound by the Vermont pattern of behavior. Surely he would drift off to what was new and exciting, leaving her behind with a shattered heart. Did you accept happiness for today, when you knew it would only bring worse pain tomorrow?

Kathryn fell asleep without reaching any decisions.

Coming downstairs the next morning, she found the object of her meditations sitting at the table in the kitchen with Nate and Amanda, having coffee. Mitchell looked rather fine-drawn, as though he hadn't had much rest himself. He was dressed casually in a dark blue shirt tucked neatly into his jeans, and he looked very much at home.

She smiled as he turned and saw her. The fiery hair, unbound for once, flowed over her shoulders. She, too, wore jeans, with a plain white cotton blouse. Mitchell stared hard at her for a moment, then rose and crossed the room to her. Putting his hands on her shoulders and bending his head, he kissed her lips tenderly. Kathryn was too conscious of her aunt and uncle's presence to respond. Stepping away from Mitchell's arms with a quick smile, she moved to the table.

"No word yet?" she asked anxiously.

Amanda poured a cup of coffee and set it down in front of her niece. "Who knows when they'll get around to it. It's the weekend, and they're probably all out playing golf."

"Now, 'Manda. The doctor said they'd do it special and he'd call me first thing this morning." Nate squeezed her hand. "He won't forget."

None of them ate much breakfast. Amanda didn't bother at all, and Nate, after a few bites of waffle drenched in maple syrup, pushed his plate away and sipped at his coffee.

When the phone rang, they all tensed. Nate rose to answer, and Amanda sat down, twisting the dish towel she was holding. Nate's face, as he stood listening, revealed little. "You're sure?" he questioned. Then, as though an invisible cloth had wiped across his lined face, it relaxed and softened. His eyes crinkled and a broad smile appeared. "Thanks a million, Doc. It's a relief to know right away. I appreciate your calling so soon." Nate's thumb and forefinger met in a victorious circle for his audience's benefit. "Yes, we're pretty glad about it, too."

When he'd hung up the phone, Nate suffered their simultaneous onslaught for a moment before begging them to desist. "What did we all get so excited about? It was just a routine thing, after all. Nothing to worry about." His eyes fastened on his wife's face, which worked with repressed emotion. "Now don't cry, honey," he begged.

Mitch drew Kathryn away. As they left the kitchen, Nate was drawing Amanda into his arms. For a moment, Mitchell and Kathryn just stood at the edge of the verandah, drinking in the fresh morning air and feeling the warmth of the sun. Kathryn wiped the last trace of tears from her cheek, and her whole face lit with the joyous release from tension.

"Let's run," she said. "Bet I can beat you!" In a flash she was off the verandah and running flat out across the back yard, her hair streaming out behind like a banner. Mitchell, after a crack of laughter, took off after her.

He let her lead the way, keeping to a position at her heels. She flew past an astounded Charlie driving heifers to the barn, past the entrance to the home garden and orchard, then swerved to run along the edge of a hay field ready for harvest. It was then Mitchell made his move, reaching out for her, touching her shoulder, slowing her. Out of breath, Kathryn allowed him to bring her to a laughing halt.

They swayed together for a moment, then collapsed into the lush growth of the hay field. "Sweetheart," he murmured huskily. As though words were inadequate, he joined his mouth to hers, his hands holding her head still for a long, trembling moment.

All around them nature teemed in her extravagant bounty. Hot sun on growing hay produced a delicious fragrance that was heady, exhilarating. Kathryn was conscious of the drone of a passing bee and the small crackling sounds of life from all around them. The fresh hay, crushed beneath them, felt springy, a bed made perfectly for lovers.

How sweet his kiss was, she thought. His hands moved softly on her throat now, tracing downward along the edge of her open collar, one finger exploring the beginning swell of her breasts. As though he needed to take in all of her at once, he ran his hands over her body from breast to thigh, burying his face in her loose hair.

"I missed you last night, Kathryn," he said finally, his voice touched with some indefinable emotion. "I can't believe I've known you such a short time. It seems like always, and yet there's so much more I want to know. I want to know you in every way that's possible between a man and a woman."

"Mitch . . ."

"I don't know if I'm like that guy you knew before. How can I say? How can I promise not to disappoint you? I'm human, with all a human's faults. If I'm arrogant and pushy at times, it's because that's how I've had to be if I didn't want to fail. Kathryn, I feel something for you I've never felt for anyone else. You must feel it, too. Otherwise you couldn't respond the way you do." His hands stilled on her waist, waiting.

Her throat tightened, and she forced herself to swallow. "I just don't know if it's what I want, Mitch. Give me some time to think about it."

His hands reluctantly released her waist, and he sighed. "Okay, honey. We've got all the time in the world."

Kathryn scrambled to her feet and stood, hands on hips, legs apart, looking at the handsome man sprawled in all his magnificent length at her feet. She allowed her eyes to feast on the rumpled hair, the lazy grin, the broad shoulders. A tremor of desire ran through her.

He shaded his eyes against the sun, looking up at her. "There's no reason you can't join me down here. We'll take our time."

She backed away from the hand held out to her in invitation. "No, I think I'd rather see how good you are as a farm boy. You have the edge at Tech Plus. Now I want to see what you can do with something that doesn't go beep-beep and do a print-out." Her chin lifted. "Do you want to accept the challenge?"

In a single, fluid motion he rose to stand close beside her. She held her ground, her eyes sparkling.

"Sure, freckle-face. Lead on. I never could resist a challenge."

She led him to the hay barn. The fragrance overwhelmed them as they entered the vast structure. It was the hay field multiplied a hundred times, a giant potpourri of all the smells of summer. Dimly lit ranks of hay bales stretched from one side to the other, almost as high as the ceiling. Kathryn pointed to a section of newer bales, freshly cut and different in color from the others.

"Now a good farm boy would be able to take one of those bales and toss it from chest level up to the top of that stack over there," she said, grinning at him mischievously. "Do you think you could do it? Be honest, now. I wouldn't want you to get a hernia."

"How much does one of those things weigh?"

"Fifty pounds."

"Stand back. If I miss, you could get flattened." He bent to grasp a bale by the strings, the muscles under his shirt rippling as he lifted it. With a movement that was only slightly awkward, he tossed the bale and it came to rest on the second rank, just above their heads. It was in place, but precariously balanced.

Her pursed lips and tilted nose spurred him to seize another bale. This one went up as easily, but the impact dislodged the first. Both bales wobbled, then came tumbling down as Kathryn and Mitchell jumped out of the way.

Kathryn laughed. "I'm not sure you could make it as a farm boy, Mitch. Even Charlie can get them to stay up better than that."

Mitchell stood with his hands on his hips, staring with disgust at the spilled contents of the broken bales. Kathryn made the mistake of giggling at him, and a gleam of mischief appeared in his green eyes to surpass her own.

"Now, Mitch," she warned as he advanced on her.

"Now, Kathryn," he mocked. "Here we have the classic situation for the farmer's daughter and the city slicker. Surely I deserve a chance to try it out." He circled around her, and she found herself backing toward the fallen hay.

"Aha, me beauty!" He twirled an imaginary mustache, his eyes glittering wickedly. When she tried to duck under his outstretched arm, he grabbed her. "This time you won't get away, my sweet. Not from Mitchell." His weight and a foot thrust behind her ankle brought them toppling over into the sweet-smelling hay.

"Oof! You great lout," she panted. "It's the bull in the hay barn, all right. Mitch!" Her cry was smothered in a great smacking kiss. When he raised his head and grinned down at her triumphantly, a wave of emotion swept over her, making her shudder.

"Kathryn!" He was instantly contrite. "Did I hurt you? I didn't mean . . ."

"Oh, Mitchell," she whispered. "Please kiss me." She didn't wait for him. Reaching up, she slid her fingers into his hair and pulled his head down to her waiting mouth, kissing him with abandon.

Her wildness was matched by his surging response. Almost desperately he threw his leg across hers and his arms strained her to him as their kiss deepened. Kathryn met him more than half way, acknowledging the need they shared.

The prickling of the almost dried hay against their bodies went unfelt. They were conscious only of two bodies seeking closer contact, searching out buttons and fastenings in their haste. Kathryn let out a shuddering sigh when she felt her naked breasts pressed against the coarse, curling hair of his chest. He moved against her, as though delighting in the sensation of the hardening, budding mounds. Her hips shifted sensuously under him as her arms tightened around his neck.

It was the sound of a tractor passing outside that brought them to a realization of their surroundings once more. Mitchell lifted his head. "This is crazy." The words were dragged out of him. "If we don't stop this now, we're going to give someone a hell of a shock when they come with the next load of hay."

Unwillingly, Kathryn's mind began to respond to his words. He had started this in fun, and she had turned it into something else. Now they were both in a state of excitement that demanded release. She opened her eyes and stared helplessly up at him, her mind in conflict with the explosive needs of her body.

"It's okay, Kathryn," he assured her, carefully lifting himself away and helping her to her feet. As she adjusted her clothing, he grinned wryly. "We're a pretty combusti-

ble pair, aren't we? I hope you take that into considera-
tion when you make your decision." His fingers worked
quickly on the buttons of his shirt. "If you make the
wrong one, I may disappear in a cloud of smoke!"

He wouldn't be the only one, Kathryn thought helplessly as she worked pieces of hay out of her hair. When
he'd finished tucking his shirt in, he helped with the task
of getting every straw out, but Kathryn knew they hadn't
been successful when, returning to the house, Amanda
took one look at her and suggested she do something
about her hair.

Kathryn took her advice and looked much neater
when she came back to the kitchen, where she found her
aunt alone.

"I hope you know what you're doing," Amanda said
without preamble, her eyes on the tidy coil at the back of
Kathryn's head.

"I hope so, too, 'Manda."

Her aunt looked tired, leaning against the counter
where she'd been kneading bread dough. "He seems like
a decent sort, Mitchell Grant. But he's lived a different
kind of life than you have, and these things"—Amanda
waved an expressive hand—"they don't mean the same
thing to men like him."

"Yes, I realize that."

"You can understand it in your head without knowing
it in your heart." Amanda glared fiercely at her. "They
don't mean to do you any harm. That's what muddies
the waters." She turned back to the dough, shoving the
heels of her hands vigorously into it. "That boy at college,
he didn't mean to do you any harm either."

Kathryn stiffened. She'd never told anyone about
Barry, but she'd always known that Amanda had
guessed. "That was a long time ago," she said softly.

"Doesn't mean it can't happen again. There's nothing
easier in the whole world than being hurt."

"You just put a bandage on it and go about your
business," Kathryn said flippantly.

Her aunt swung around, her eyes narrowed. *"That's* the bandage you applied—trying to turn everything into a joke. Oh, you weren't going to take anything seriously anymore, were you, Kathryn? Life was going to be had only on your terms, with a laugh and a shrug. Well, that's no way to shield yourself from the realities of life. There *are* important things, serious things, and acting as though there weren't doesn't make it so."

"I'm trying to face that," Kathryn admitted, her hands twining nervously behind her back. "But this is all very confusing to me. I love him, 'Manda."

Her aunt winced slightly before giving Kathryn an encouraging smile. "Well, maybe it will work out for the best. Under all that teasing you're a level-headed woman. We're here if you need us."

"Thanks."

"Run along now." Amanda placed her flour-covered hands once again on the bread dough. "Dinner's at the usual time."

Kathryn wanted to be alone, and she wandered around the farm, feeling suddenly like a stranger in the place she'd loved so well. Such a short time away, and she didn't seem to fit in anymore. Nate had been right. She knew now she would never be happy living a life like Margaret's. Her mind had been stimulated by working with Jim Zachary; it had been challenged by Mitchell's forcing her to prove herself. She would always love the country, be refreshed and renewed by coming back from time to time, but she needed more now.

There was an apple tree in the orchard that was a special favorite of hers. Larger than all the others, she knew from experience that its gnarled trunk and branches were just right for climbing and sitting in. She hauled herself up now, grabbing one of the ripened apples.

Nate and Mitchell came around the corner of the house, talking. Kathryn knew from the way her heart seemed to swell that what she needed was Mitchell.

Whether she could live with his arrogance and his ruthlessness, she didn't know. He was often tender with her, even thoughtful. But would that last? When he was sure of her, would he treat her in the same calculating manner he did all his business affairs? He was a man who planned to go far. It didn't seem likely he would want to take her with him all the way.

"What are you doing up there?"

Her dark musings were interrupted. Mitchell stood beneath the tree, looking up at her.

She took another bite of her apple and chewed it, looking gravely back. "Want a bite?" she asked, holding it out to him.

"I don't believe this." The sunlight fell through the tree's branches on the faint sprinkling of his freckles. "Come on down, Eve. It's time for dinner, then we have to hit the road. You can bring some of those with you, if you want." He held up his arms, and she slid down into them. For a moment he held her suspended above the ground.

"Don't drop me," she cautioned.

"I wouldn't dare," he replied. "I've just had a talk with your uncle. It can best be summed up by saying that if I don't take good care of you, I might as well go back to that mountain in Colorado and jump off—without a rope."

"They worry about me." He let her slide to the ground, and she met his gaze. "But I'm a woman now, and I have to take care of myself."

"With my help, I hope." He kissed her on the tip of her nose, then once lightly on the lips. "I've only just begun to take care of you, Kathryn. We're going to spend a lot of time together back in Boston, because nothing can keep us apart!"

11

⚬⚬⚬⚬⚬⚬⚬⚬⚬⚬⚬

Two inches of newstype in the business section of the
Boston Globe made chaos of their plans.

Kathryn was just taking the dust cover off her terminal
when Mitchell came out of the stairway, moving fast. He
held a newspaper clenched in his hand and hardly
seemed to notice her as he charged into Jim's office.

"What the hell is this, Jim?" His voice rang harshly.
"Who's been talking?" The door closed, leaving Kathryn
staring in astonishment.

Several employees were grouped around a newspaper
down the hall. Kathryn joined them to find out what all
the fuss was about.

"An important new advance in security systems is
being rumored in software circles," she read. "The
system allegedly is un-crackable, and will have enormous
impact in this crucial field. . . . Mitchell Grant, head of
Technology Plus, the firm which purportedly has devel-
oped the program, was unavailable for comment at this
printing."

Jim's door flew open and Mitchell emerged, his face hard and set. As he strode toward the stairway, Kathryn reached out to touch his arm. He glanced at her briefly but only murmured, "Later, Kathryn," before he was gone.

After a moment she hesitantly moved to Jim's doorway. He was sitting at his desk, the newspaper open in front of him, a dazed look on his face. His head jerked up when she spoke his name.

"I didn't say anything to Roger . . . or anyone else," he insisted.

"Of course not."

"Mitch seems to think it was either Rita or me who spilled the beans. Hell, I spent the whole day Saturday with her and Roger on his boat, and the only thing he tried to do was hire me away from here. Mitch has gotten it into his head that Rita's some kind of Mata Hari. Can't he see she's not at all like that?"

"He'll see it when he calms down," Kathryn said, but her voice lacked assurance, and she moved off to her cubicle feeling deeply disturbed.

Though she went past Mitchell's office several times that day, she found the door closed. She observed that Susan was bombarded with phone calls from wire services and technology newsletters that had picked up on the news item.

"As well as corporate bigwigs he's been dealing with," Susan confided. "They're ticked off about the news leaking prematurely. He's been on the phone or with staff all day."

At five Kathryn found a diffident Rita waiting by the elevator. Jim emerged from his office, looking defiant, and took Rita's arm as the doors opened. Kathryn smiled encouragingly at them before going to her cubicle to gather up her purse and coat. Downstairs Susan was gone for the day, but Mitchell's door was still closed. She tapped lightly.

"Come in."

He lifted weary eyes as she entered, but his expression immediately softened. Kathryn moved swiftly to where he sat behind his desk and slid her arms around his neck, preventing him from rising. "Remember me?" she asked, pressing a kiss on his lips. His arms rose automatically to enclose her. He returned her kiss as he drew her onto his lap. After a moment Kathryn let her head drop to his shoulder, her body relaxing against him. They sat that way for some time without speaking.

At last he said huskily, "I needed that." His arms tightened, drawing her comfortably closer.

"So did I." She nuzzled into his neck. "It's been a rough day, hasn't it?"

His chest lifted with a heavy sigh. "Yes. There was no way to plan for something like this." His mouth quirked ruefully. "So much for my resolution to prove you were wrong about me. Can you bear with me?"

"I'll have to, won't I?" Gathering her courage, she said, "Jim was very upset this morning."

Mitchell's arms clenched, causing Kathryn to protest. He released her, and she reluctantly left his lap. Rising himself, he began to pace restlessly.

"He shouldn't be. He can write his own ticket with any software firm in the country, now the word is out. Or he could get backing to start out on his own again."

"I don't think he'll do that . . . unless you drive him to it."

"I'm not driving; that woman is pulling."

"Rita? Her interest in him is personal, not professional."

The cynical smile he gave her made her heart sink. "She got him out on Roger's boat, didn't she?"

"You know Jim's crazy about boats. If he wanted to spend a little time with her on Roger's boat, it wasn't because there's any danger of him leaving Tech Plus."

"And yet the news item appeared right after their cozy day together."

"It wouldn't be in Roger's interest for the news to get

167

out. Or Rita's, for that matter. Something this important was bound to leak out. If you thought Rita had done it, you'd have fired her."

"What would be the point?" he demanded. "She already knows everything there is to know about the program. I've made it clear she'll be slapped with a lawsuit if she's involved with the development of a similar program anywhere else. So she finishes her contract with me, and I've told Jim to keep strictly to business with her."

"Mitchell!" Kathryn was appalled. "You can't tell Jim how to run his personal life."

Some of the old arrogance cooled his eyes as he regarded her flushed face. "Kathryn, you'll have to trust my judgment on this. The future of my business is at stake here. It's going to take time getting through this mess, and I'll need all the support I can get."

He opened his arms to her and she walked into them. Dropping his head to rest on the shining crown of her hair, he murmured in a tired voice, "Stick with me, Kathryn. This is when I need your help."

"I'm here," she whispered, though her heart ached even as his lips urgently sought hers.

But he didn't give her much opportunity to give him support over the next few days. It was a hectic period, marked by unease among the staff, flying rumors, and short tempers. Mitch appeared grim and unapproachable, and his relations with Jim were strained. Kathryn longed to do something about it, and finally, since he made no effort to see her, appeared in his office.

Her hands were on her hips and her tone was no-nonsense. "Mitchell Grant, you have an appointment with Kathryn Lambert at one o'clock. For lunch. I trust that doesn't conflict with anything else on your schedule, because if it does, I'll expect you to unconflict it."

He put down his pen, the tired lines around his eyes relaxing. A sudden grin appeared, the first she'd seen in days. "Since you put it that way, I'll have to fit you in."

His eyes were alight with the expression she loved, really seeing her again. "We might have to make it a long lunch hour."

"That's perfectly acceptable to me," she said primly, abruptly vanishing from his office.

Before meeting him, she checked her appearance in the restroom mirror. Excitement had brought back the sparkle in her eyes and heightened the color in her cheeks; she needed nothing further in the way of makeup except a touch of lipstick. She slipped on the jacket of her suit, a light-weight tweed in browns and blues. It would go nicely anywhere he cared to take her for lunch.

Mitchell was waiting for her as the elevator doors swished open on the ground floor. Reaching in, he drew her out and tucked her arm under his, smiling down at her.

"I don't believe it," she said, mocking him. "I was sure I'd have to drag you out of your office."

"I've been counting the minutes. There's a place on Newbury that serves a terrific baked stuffed flounder . . ."

Kathryn heaved a sigh. "I see. Counting the minutes 'til your lunch."

He only squeezed her hand and smiled.

They were led to a booth in the back corner of the restaurant. Even in the dim light she could see how intently he was observing her, his eyes warm with yearning. Though he said little, she could feel his need in the touch of his hand, stroking hers lightly under the table on her knee. The baked flounder was produced almost too soon.

"This is delicious," she reported enthusiastically. "I can see the fatal attraction of this place."

"The fatal attraction here is you."

She felt a little nervous under his steady gaze. "Well, I've been compared to a chair; there's no reason I shouldn't be compared to a stuffed flounder."

He paused in lifting his glass of wine. "I love your

169

quirky sense of humor, Kathryn, but right now I want you to take me seriously. These are real emotions we're dealing with—the way we feel about each other."

"Yes, I know," she said softly. "Amanda warned me about the jokes when I was in Vermont."

"She's a shrewd woman, your aunt."

Kathryn nodded, but she was remembering Amanda's concern that Mitch's feelings, though real, were probably temporary. She met his piercing green eyes and offered a nervous smile. "I'm trying to be honest with myself."

"Good." He lifted his glass in a toast. "To the very lovely and very patient woman who has lured me into the most dangerous arena of all."

Though he offered it as a compliment, and used their private joke about matadors and bullrings to amuse her, his toast was more disturbing than pleasing to Kathryn. It suggested his being drawn against his will, and that loving was a dangerous game. A temporary game? She told herself she was reading too much into his words, but the tension remained with her throughout the meal, despite her efforts to dispel it.

He was more attuned to her mood than she expected. As they finished, he cocked his head at her questioningly. "Is it that we haven't been able to spend much time together? I'll call the office and tell them not to expect us back this afternoon."

"Oh, no," she protested. "You probably have important things to do."

"Nothing more important than being with you."

He was adamant, and she found herself walking with him, aimlessly at first, and then more purposefully toward the Quincy Market. They talked as they walked—about inconsequential things, their likes and dislikes, anecdotes from earlier years. At Fanueil Hall the succulent odors of food surrounded them, and they browsed through dozens of specialty shops: flowers, clothing, souvenirs, crafts, antiques, books. Mitch bought Brie and bread and wine. "For later," he said, grinning at her.

His good humor was so firmly in place that Kathryn gradually worked up the nerve to introduce the one topic that most nagged at her. They were looking through a selection of woven wool scarves and he was teasing that they'd have to match her eyes, when she asked abruptly, "Could we talk about Jim?"

A reserved look shuttered his face. "Jim will do what he wants. I can't stop him."

Kathryn shrugged her shoulders impatiently. "Jim has no intention of leaving Tech Plus. Not unless you make him choose between the company and Rita, that is. He's loyal to the company, but he's loyal to her, too. Your suspicions about her are very upsetting to him."

"She works for Roger Owens."

"Rita doesn't care two pins for Roger or technological piracy, or anything like that. She simply likes Jim. If you'd seen them together, like I have, you'd *know* those two were meant for each other."

His look was rueful. "You're a romantic, Kathryn. Aren't you maybe seeing them through your own rose-colored glasses?"

She tossed the scarves back on the table, exasperated. "You know a lot about computers and a lot about corporations, but *I* know a lot about people. And I don't need a crystal ball to tell those two are in love."

A clerk had stopped at Mitch's elbow to ask if he wanted the scarf he was holding, one of swirling brown tones with brilliant cobalt blue. He nodded absently, digging in a pocket for his wallet. His thoughts were obviously not on the scarf, but on what Kathryn had been saying.

"Are you sure you want that?" she asked.

"It's for you." He accepted his change and handed the plastic bag to her.

"Thank you." Kathryn didn't know whether to laugh or cry.

He guided her out of the shop and bent to kiss her. "Maybe you're right about Jim and Rita," he said, a little gruffly. "I'm too close to the problem to be objective. It just seemed awfully convenient, that attraction coming when it did."

"I've learned you can't always help an attraction when it happens to you," she said softly.

He touched the tip of her nose, almost with regret, she thought. "That's true. All right, I'll talk to Jim tomorrow."

Relieved, she gave him a quick hug. He glanced at his watch and said, "Great. It's past closing time. You won't have any objection to going to my penthouse now, will you?"

"None," she assured him, her heart feeling lighter than it had in days.

When they arrived at the penthouse floor, Kathryn stepped inside the foyer and grimaced as she caught sight of her unruly hair in a tall mirror. An Oriental runner cushioned her tired feet as she followed Mitchell into the living room, where she was struck by the colorful carpet —a glowing sapphire blue with creamy tones woven into the stylized Persian design. Her eyes traveled to the cream-colored sofas that stood against walls of exposed brick.

"So this is the lair of the tyrant of Tech Plus," she teased, not wanting to sound too naively impressed.

A small tree was tucked into the corner between the sofas, saving the room from looking overly formal. The rippling sound of water drew her, and she turned to find a mass of greenery banked around a metal sculpture. Its construction allowed water to flow from one level to another, creating a miniature waterfall. That Mitchell would invest in Oriental rugs didn't surprise Kathryn; that he would create such a fresh and restful haven told her something new about him.

Her glowing eyes told him how much she liked it, but before she could speak, the phone rang. Mitchell walked over to the connection module and pulled it, silencing the ring.

"No phones tonight," he said, smiling. "And it's not time for dinner, so how about a shower? Mine's a lot sturdier than yours; it will hold both of us."

"I could be convinced."

"How?" he asked, capturing her in a fervent embrace.

When he released her, she said breathlessly, "That was a good start."

"I have a great middle, too, and a spectacular finish."

"Show me."

"What you need for a proper shower is two naked bodies," he informed her, as he grasped her hand and led her toward the bedroom. It was lit only by the lights of the city through one large window at the side of the room, but she could clearly see his hands as they came to cup her breasts through the light suit jacket. Kathryn began to wonder if they would make it to the shower.

He slowly unbuttoned her jacket and then her blouse, hanging each carefully over the back of a chair. Then he caressed her breasts through the cotton bra, but made no effort to remove it. Instead he removed his own clothes, right down to his shorts.

"God, I could spend my life undressing you," he murmured, running his hands down the length of her body. "Uncovering that glorious skin is a life-long labor of love." His fingers came to the snap and zipper of her skirt, releasing them and easing the fabric down to her feet, so she could step out of it.

Kathryn kicked off her shoes, her breath already coming a little raggedly. "Are you sure you want a shower?"

"Positive." His hands were at the waist of her pantyhose, carefully moving it downward, his fingers straying to stroke the tops of her thighs and between her legs. When she shuddered with pleasure, he kissed her with increasing passion. But after a moment he drew back. "This won't do," he said firmly, returning to the removal of her pantyhose. "You have to see my bathroom."

She followed him through the door into a room that

was at least as large as her living room. As she surveyed the luxurious appointments, he turned on the water and steam billowed over the clear glass door. His hands slid behind her and unfastened the bra, removing it quickly and hanging it over a towel rack. Then he took off his shorts and drew her to him, pressing her against his naked body, already hard with desire.

"Into the shower, or we'll never make it," he groaned.

The water splashed against her skin, beating in rhythm with the excitement that coursed through her. He soaped his hands and rubbed them over her, over every inch of her waiting, thrilling flesh. More shyly, she did the same, marveling at the fine texture of his skin and the coarseness of his hair. And then they were laughing, the tensions running too high to be handled any other way, their mirth mingled with long, lingering kisses.

He dried her with a fluffy towel that became only an extension of his hands, exploring, soothing, exciting in turns. Her head felt almost dizzy from the steam and the mounting desire. When she had toweled him off, he led her back to the bedroom and enclosed her in his arms, as he lay down on the bed. She snuggled against him, a sweet urgency pulsing through her. She was immensely aware of the feel of his naked body pressing hers, of her breasts against the roughness of his masculine chest.

Her eyes were luminous in the half-light as he trailed his mouth downwards, cherishing her with his lips as well as his hands. He embraced her tenderest flesh with his tongue and scattered kisses against her warm skin. Then, with the grace of a dancer, he lifted her onto him, to lavish her breasts with suckling kisses. Her whole body surged toward him in an abandonment of passion. "Oh, Mitchell, I need you so much . . ."

The joining of their bodies brought her shivering to the brink of ecstasy. His mouth covered her moistly parted lips, his tongue duplicating the rhythm of their bodies. Kathryn was roused to such a feverish pitch that the shuddering of his body in release sent her soaring over the brink to come gliding, gliding down to his arms.

His hands still molded her hips against him, his lips brushing her face repeatedly. "You're the most incredible thing that's ever happened to me, Kathryn."

She was still too shaken by the experience to speak. With her fingers she followed the contours of his dearly loved face. A quip surfaced in her mind, but she thrust it aside. This time she wouldn't hide behind some frivolous remark. "I won't ever regret meeting you," she whispered. "No matter what happens. You're the most vital, enchanting man I've ever met."

"Only good things are going to happen," he assured her, his arms drawing her protectively against him.

"I put an English muffin in the toaster for you," he said the next morning when she joined him in the spacious kitchen. "There are eggs if you want them, but I should get on downstairs." He stood leaning against the counter, a mug of coffee in his hand.

"I don't want to take you away from your business, Mitch. I just want to share you." The muffin popped up, and she slathered it with butter.

"Yesterday's break was just what I needed," he admitted. "Not just the break—being with you."

The breath caught in her throat, but she managed to lean across and kiss him. "You go ahead. I'll be downstairs in a minute."

"Okay. You're going to start the debugging for Jim, aren't you?"

She nodded and waved him off, wanting a moment by herself to absorb everything that had happened in the last twenty-four hours. Her heart was bursting with an almost painful ecstasy. Love had never come to her so overwhelmingly before.

The episode with Barry—well, it looked like youthful infatuation compared to this. Mitch was the most wonderful man she'd ever met. And he'd accepted her judgment about Jim. Surely nothing was more essential to a loving relationship than that kind of trust.

When she'd finished the English muffin, she rode down in the elevator, envying Mitchell's convenient commute. At the second floor she stepped out into the dark, silent lobby and flipped on the lights. Whistling a Stephen Foster tune, she strode happily to her cubicle and turned on the terminal. Then she opened the locked cabinet that contained the disks she needed. Her whistling stopped abruptly.

There was nothing on the shelf where the disks were always kept. But she remembered immediately that she'd left early and decided Jim must have put them somewhere else. After searching for several minutes, however, she had to conclude that they weren't in the cabinet or in Jim's or Rita's offices. When she couldn't think of anyplace else to look, she picked up the intercom.

"Mitch, I can't locate the security program disks. Did you give new instructions for storing them?"

"No." His voice was tense. "I'll be right there."

He arrived so quickly she knew he'd taken the stairs instead of the elevator. "I didn't mean to alarm you," she said, "but I've looked everywhere. Of course, no one can access the material on the disks without knowing the special code."

"It's the documentation that matters. Did you check the safe to see if the copy's there?"

She shook her head. "Only you and Jim have the combination."

She was right behind him as he strode to the computer room and unlocked the door. By the time she got the light switched on, he was crouched in front of the safe, clearing the tumblers. His jaw was clenched, but then, her own breathing was rapid and irregular. She held her breath as the door swung open.

Empty. It took only a split second to see that, yet they

both stood transfixed, staring at the bare shelves. After the first instant of shock, Mitchell's face contorted into an ugly grimace, and he pounded his fist helplessly against the barren safe.

Kathryn felt numb. A dazed question came out of her mouth. "Who could have taken it?"

Mitchell swung around and rasped, "It had to be Jim or me. Take your pick."

"It could have been an outsider."

"An outsider with the key and the combination? Talk sense, Kathryn. At any rate, I've probably ruined any fingerprints on the knobs."

Fingerprints. The word sounded wretchedly grim to Kathryn. "Please don't jump to conclusions. Jim should be here in a few minutes."

His eyes were held by hers for a long moment. "I'll watch for him downstairs."

Without another word he slammed the safe door closed, and locked the computer room behind them. Kathryn returned to her desk, worried. The warm glow she'd felt in his kitchen was long gone. Not that she believed for a minute that Jim or Rita was guilty of any wrongdoing. She just wished they'd show up.

Other employees arrived on time, but Jim and Rita didn't come. It occurred to her that Mitchell had waylaid them downstairs. She called Susan, only to learn that neither of them had arrived yet.

At half past nine Mitchell walked into her cubicle. His face was set into hard lines, and he sat down close to her so he could keep his voice lowered. "No one knows what's going on, and I want to keep it that way as long as I can. I've called Jim's apartment and Rita's. There's no answer at either place. I don't like the fact that she's missing, too."

"What are you going to do?"

"Call the police. What else can I do?"

"The police!" Her voice rose and Mitchell touched her lips with a fingertip. "Jim's not a criminal."

"Then why isn't he here this morning? Why hasn't he called?"

"Give him time!"

His hoarse whisper was packed with intensity. "Time for what? Kathryn, I've been robbed. The longer I wait, the more damage can be done. Try seeing it from my point of view."

Kathryn strained forward, longing to offer the support he was asking for. "Mitch, I know this is terrible for you. Please don't feel I'm against you just because I expect Jim to show up and explain everything."

Mitchell stood up. If her plea touched him, it didn't show on his face. "Well, he'd better show soon. I'll give him another half hour."

Nothing happened to alleviate her concern during that time. Just before the deadline she picked up her jacket and purse and walked down to his office. The door was open and she walked in and closed it behind her. "Don't call the police, Mitchell."

His voice was like steel. "Why not?"

"You know Jim as well as I do. He simply wouldn't do anything dishonest."

"I can't run a business that way."

"We're not talking about a business. We're talking about people! You have to give a man like Jim the benefit of the doubt. At least for a few hours."

His jaw was set. "Every minute may count against me, Kathryn. You're asking me to risk everything—Tech Plus, everybody's jobs, the Beresfords' money—on how you feel about Jim. I can't do that." He picked up the phone. "You can't always trust your feelings."

She watched him start to tap out the number, each digit making her feel more frozen. "Maybe you're right. I certainly shouldn't have trusted my feelings about you!"

Without another word she turned on her heel and rushed out of the office onto Boylston Street, into a life without Mitchell Grant.

12

For the next hour Kathryn walked without purpose or direction. She found herself on an approach overlooking the Charles River and seated herself on one of the benches in a miniature park. A flight of leaves, colored in russet and dull golds, fluttered in front of her, carried by a sudden breeze.

At this sign of autumn in the city, Kathryn sighed, wondering where she would be when the first snow came. Back on the farm? No. That would be going back for all the wrong reasons. Surely she had come to a point where she knew who she was. It was simply a matter of finding a place to be that person . . . without Mitch. The dull ache around her heart expanded into a sharp pain.

A city bus approached a nearby bus stop. Its destination sign indicated that it should take her somewhere near Jim Zachary's apartment. On an impulse she swung aboard and questioned the driver. At his affirmative answer, she dropped into an empty seat and began

179

watching street signs. She wondered if she'd see police cars outside Jim's building.

Everything was quiet in the neighborhood. There was no answer at Jim's door. His was the only mail slot with a delivery in it, so she assumed it was from the previous day. At a loss for what to do next, Kathryn decided she might as well go home. She felt rumpled and sticky in the clothes she'd worn all the previous day.

The pain hit her again as she remembered why she was still wearing yesterday's outfit. Oh, God. How long did this intense pain last?

A bus drew up on the corner, but it wasn't the one she wanted. Across the street a car screeched to a halt and a door slammed. She looked toward the sound and saw Mitchell striding toward her. Instinctively she jumped onto the bus just as the doors were closing and hung onto the metal upright by the fare box as the vehicle lurched away from the curb. The driver ignored the pounding of Mitch's fist on the door. The last Kathryn saw as they went around the corner was his tall figure plunging angrily back toward the Mercedes.

Panicking at the thought he might come after her, she had no sooner paid her fare than she got off again. She simply couldn't face Mitchell yet. His car wasn't in sight, so she ran along a side street and ducked into a mom-and-pop store on one corner, her heart palpitating madly. Through the dusty, cluttered window she searched the street, but no Mercedes went by. After a considerable length of time, she bought a candy bar and ventured cautiously out of the shop. In a while she found a cruising cab to take her back to her apartment.

When she unlocked her door and went in, she felt bone weary. Dropping her purse on the table by the door, she headed for the bedroom where she undressed and picked up the flowered batiste robe. Almost shaking from nerves and exhaustion, she filled the ancient tub and climbed in for a long soak.

The phone rang, unanswered, three separate times before she finally got out of the bath. Her skin was still damp as she put on the robe, and the thin fabric felt cool on her skin as it dried. Her hair she left twisted up in a knot on top of her head. There was no reason to get dressed, so she lay down on the bed to rest. The phone rang again.

After the fourth ring, she reached for it, on the suddenly inspired thought that it might be Jim. If it was Mitch, she would just hang up.

"Hi, Kathryn. Is Mitch there?"

"No, but he's trying to find you."

"Yes, well, I've been trying to find *him*." Jim sounded far away and almost annoyed. "But he's not in the office. Susan thought he might be at your place."

"Jim, do you have the security program and the documentation?"

"Sure. That's why I wanted to get in touch with him, so he wouldn't worry. We tried to call last night."

With a pang Kathryn remembered the unanswered ringing of the phone in Mitch's apartment. "Mitch has been frantic. Why did you take it?"

Jim sighed. "It's a long story. Roger actually tried to bribe Rita yesterday. And my keys were missing for a while when we were out on his boat last Saturday. I know it sounds very cloak-and-daggerish, but I'm beginning to think it wouldn't be past Roger to make an impression of a key and have someone break into Tech Plus, you know? We really should have the locks changed. Anyway, we just thought we'd take all the stuff with us for safekeeping. Of course, we expected to be back there first thing this morning."

Kathryn was shaking her head in astonishment. "Why weren't you?"

"We spent the night out of town, just on a whim." He sounded a little embarrassed at this point, but continued bravely. "We'd arranged to go before all this came up.

Then this morning when we were headed back to work my car broke down in the middle of nowhere. I tried to call Mitch as soon as we got anywhere near a phone."

"Oh, Jim." Kathryn couldn't make herself tell him about Mitch calling the police. "Try him again at the office, and if he's not there, leave a message that you've told me all about it. I'll explain if he calls me. You should just try to get back to town."

"Okay. The thing is, Kathryn, I didn't want Mitch blaming Rita if Roger did try anything."

"Yes, I can see that."

Kathryn sat staring at the receiver after he'd hung up. That was it. The big mystery solved. She sighed. And where was Mitchell? Downtown, arranging charges against Jim? Grief pierced her as she remembered Mitch's agreeing the previous day to trust her judgment about Jim and Rita. Tears slid unnoticed down her cheeks.

It made no difference that Jim and Rita were in the clear. Mitchell had made his decision. Even if he had to acknowledge jumping to the wrong conclusion this time, he would always put his drive to succeed ahead of personal values. It was better that she accepted that now.

The doorbell rang. She knew it would be Mitchell. She had no choice but to let him in, of course, and convey Jim's message. When she opened the door he just stood there, leaning with one hand braced on the wall. He stared steadily at her, his face expressionless as his finger dropped from the doorbell. She stepped aside silently and he walked in.

"We have to talk." His eyes rested on her strained face.

Drawing a deep breath, Kathryn nodded. "Yes. About the missing files—"

He interrupted her. "Why did you run away? From the office and from Jim's?"

She stared at him, then spoke carefully. "I think we covered that this morning. I'm sorry about jumping on the bus. It was a childish impulse, but I really didn't want to talk to you then. About the program, Jim—"

"To hell with Jim!"

"Listen to me!" she insisted, managing, before he could start in again, to catch his attention and blurt out the whole story. Her voice finally died away and the defiant expression in her eyes faded. Feeling slightly weak in the knees, she abruptly sat down on the sofa and turned her head away from him. She felt the cushions give as he sat down next to her.

"Well? Aren't you going to say something?" she asked.

"So that's what it was? I should have figured on something hair-brained like that, knowing Jim." His arm was along the back of the sofa, and she turned to find him facing her.

Kathryn stared at him. "You certainly should have! You do know Jim."

"But I don't know Rita."

"To call in the police like that! You could have waited."

He grinned at her. "So I'm a little hot-tempered. If you'd waited another minute, you'd have seen that I never finished the call. When I turned around, you were gone."

"Well, your business is safe. That's all that really matters," she said bitterly.

"We have an issue between us to deal with."

"There's no point, Mitch."

"There's every point, Kathryn. One thing I've learned is that there are problems along the way to anything worth achieving. You have to deal with them as they come up."

She stirred restlessly, her fingers plucking the fabric of her robe. "We look at things too differently, Mitch."

"We wouldn't have been so attracted to each other if we didn't have a lot in common." He shrugged. "As for the differences, that's what it's all about, isn't it? We complement one another. I like the way your mind works, and I enjoy sparring with you."

Kathryn clasped her hands in her lap and fixed her gaze on them. "I'm afraid I might let myself be talked into something I really don't want. Since I came to work for you, I've seen how a lot of personal values get lost when it comes to getting ahead. You can be so rough and uncaring at work, and it's hard to reconcile that to the way you are with me."

His hand covered hers, and his thumb rubbed gently across the backs of her folded hands. His voice was reflective, serious. "Recently I've tried to see things from your viewpoint, as well as my own, because I love you and don't want to lose you."

Kathryn felt a shock run through her. To hear him voice it as a simple statement of fact affected her profoundly. She tried not to let it sway her, but her blue eyes clung to his as he went on.

"My business means a lot to me. I've worked hard to build it up, and I don't like to see anything threaten it. But I care about the people who work for me, and I feel responsible for them. If I'm also aggressive and goal-oriented, well, that's the way I am. I don't regret it. You have to have a little faith, Kathryn. Don't you think you're letting the way you felt about that other guy color the way you see me?"

"Mitch, I . . ." She paused, uncertain of her conviction. Had she actually been superimposing Barry's character on what she knew of Mitchell's? Certainly she had found differences. Maybe she had been attributing bad motives where none existed. The smooth charm he had used to ease the situation with Nate and Amanda could have been the only way he knew to help her, not a manipulative tactic based on self-interest. She thought of his tenderness that day on the farm—and all the other times.

That certainly wasn't ruthlessness. If he had a temper and made arrogant assumptions, well . . .

Seeing her hesitation, he pressed his advantage. "Okay, so we haven't known each other very long. You

don't think I expected things to move this fast, do you?"
His voice dropped huskily, and he was suddenly very
near, his arms sliding around her, pulling her close.
"Kathryn, sweetheart, you hit me like a bomb almost
from the first. You affected my judgment and my temper,
to say nothing of my sleep."

He pulled her onto his lap so her head was resting on
his shoulder. His mouth touched the softness of her lips,
and he kissed her with a distracted urgency, as though he
couldn't bear being near her another moment without
doing so. Kathryn could recognize the impulse, because it
was identical to her own. There was no denying the
intensity of her reactions to him, both physical and
emotional. This man meant more to her than anything
else in the world.

After a moment he drew back to look deeply into her
eyes. "What I'm trying to say is that my so-called goals
aren't going to mean a whole lot unless you're with me. I
never figured any woman could make that much difference, but then I never figured a red-headed farmer's
daughter would come into my life and turn it upside
down."

"No more than I expected a software entrepreneur to
sweep me off my feet," she said, smiling softly. "It feels
so right being in your arms. But what are we going to do
about it?"

"We're going to get married, of course," he informed
her with what sounded like the old arrogance, but there
was a twinkle in his green eyes. He brushed his fingers
along the side of her face and smiled down at her with a
tenderness that made her eyes mist. "I love you, Kathryn. With everything I have and with everything I am."
His voice rang with sincerity. "I may not be perfect, but
I'll try to make you happy. There's nothing I want to have
that doesn't include you and what you want, too."

Kathryn tightened her arms around his beloved neck.
"Oh, I do love you," she whispered.

His hands hovered over her lightly clad body, just

touching the shape of her breasts and tracing the opening of her robe. Her flesh quivered, responding instinctively to the tantalizing contact, and she smiled mistily. "The day I met you on the farm and accepted the job at Tech Plus, I wondered if I'd made the biggest mistake of my life. Funny. It turns out to be the best decision I've ever made."

Her lips met his, trembling slightly in her happiness and growing need. The stroking of his hands had descended to the inner curves of her lap, calling forth a familiar and yet strangely new burgeoning of desire.

"Next to agreeing to marry me," he prompted.

As he pushed apart the robe to expose her body, she grinned. "Yes. Next to that."

SPECIAL ANNOUNCEMENT

From January 1985 new titles in the Silhouette Romance and First Love Series will be. available (in the U.K.) from Silhouette Reader Service only.

If you have enjoyed reading these books or would like to try one please write for details of exciting offers to:

**Silhouette Reader Service,
FREEPOST
P.O. Box 236,
Croydon,
Surrey. CR9 9EL
(you don't even need a stamp)**

Silhouette Desire

COMING NEXT MONTH

MOON ON EAST MOUNTAIN
Hope McIntyre

THROUGH LAUGHTER AND TEARS
Marie Nicole

DREAM BUILDER
Naomi Horton

Silhouette Desire

FEBRUARY TITLES

THE WRONG MAN
Ann Major

SWEETHEART OF A DEAL
Suzanne Michelle

DANIELLE'S DOLL
Angel Milan

PROMISE OF LOVE
Ariel Berk

ODDS AGAINST
Erin Ross

MAID IN BOSTON
Paula Corbett

Silhouette Special Edition

FEBRUARY TITLES

F5897

Silhouette Desire

Your chance to write back!

We'll send you details of an exciting free offer from *SILHOUETTE*, if you can help us by answering the few simple questions below.

Just fill in this questionnaire, tear it out and put it in an envelope and post today to: Silhouette Reader Survey, FREEPOST, P.O. Box 236, Croydon, Surrey CR9 9EL. You don't even need a stamp.

What is the title of the *SILHOUETTE Desire* you have just read?

_____

How much did you enjoy it?

Very much ☐   Quite a lot ☐   Not very much ☐

Would you buy another *SILHOUETTE Desire* book?

Yes ☐   Possibly ☐   No ☐

How did you discover *SILHOUETTE Desire* books?

Advertising ☐   A friend ☐   Seeing them on sale ☐

Elsewhere (please state) _____

How often do you read romantic fiction?

Frequently ☐   Occasionally ☐   Rarely ☐

Name (Mrs/Miss) _____

Address _____

_____

_____ **Postcode** _____

Age group: Under 24 ☐   25–34 ☐   35–44 ☐

45–55 ☐   Over 55 ☐

Silhouette Reader Service, P.O. Box 236, Croydon, Surrey CR9 9EL.

SD1